In Defe

Written by:

Ron L. Carter and H.R. Carter

Copyright 2019 by Ron L. Carter and H.R. Carter

***

Published at Smashwords

***

Smashwords Edition, license notes

***

Disclaimer

The people and places appearing in this book, as well as the story, are fictitious. Any resemblance to real people, living or dead, is entirely coincidental.

***

Table of Contents

Prelude

There are real monsters on this earth, but for fear of them, no sane person likes to admit that it's true.

In our oceans, there are sharks that lurk in the shadows of the depths of the ocean that are 20 feet long and weigh up to 2,000 pounds. With their grossly jagged teeth, they can devour their prey with a single bite. If you get caught in the waters when they are feeding, they can rip an arm or leg from your body as they continue to eat you.

In the African plains, there are lions that weigh up to 800 pounds and are eleven feet long, from nose to tip of the tail. They are fiercely violent, and with their sharp claws and teeth, they can rip a body to pieces. If you cross their path, they will kill you and eat you.

There are huge Tigers in the wild that are over eleven feet long and weigh up to 600 pounds. They can wrap themselves around you, and with their razor-sharp claws and gruesome strangulation bites to the neck, they can kill you and eat you.

There are the bears that grow to a height of twelve feet in the forests that weighs up to 1600 pounds with a head that is 27" wide. With their massive arms and six-inch razor-sharp claws, they can rip through a person's body like butter. With one swoop, they can remove a person's arm or leg and then continue to eat you while you are still alive.

If these monsters weren't bad enough, there are the human monsters that are hidden in society. They take special delight in torturing, sometimes mutilating and killing their victims: sometimes they eat you.

And still, yet, there are the monsters that are hidden deep within our minds that we fear. When we go to bed at night, we lie there and pray that none of those monsters will ever become part of our reality.

Oh yes, there are monsters in this world.

On a dark and hidden mountain at an altitude of approximately 6400 feet near the outer banks of the Snake River lies the Mount Skokomish Wilderness of the Olympic National forest. The sun was starting to peek through the trees when a massive creature crouched behind a large tree was eyeing a mule deer: dinner, no doubt. The prey was quick and fast but no match against the creature's speed and agility. Its attack was swift and deadly, and its fury was stealth. It left behind the mutilated carcass and rib bones that bore strong striations of teeth marks as it tried to get the last morsels of flesh. Much like the bite of a human but much, much wider.

Chapter 1 - The Sighting

Zakary (Zak) Thomas was finishing his third beer. It was 5:30, and he was feeling a little tipsy. He knew he had to pick up dinner before he headed home. "Best stop now, dude," he thought. "Set the microbrew down, pay your check, hit the head, then get home."

Zak had been home from Afghanistan for about a year and had recently gotten a job with the state of Washington Forestry Department as a forest ranger. He was married but had been separated for a few months from his wife, Julie. She was his high school sweetheart, and they married just before he began his stint with the United States Army. She was athletic, outgoing blond, five feet six inches tall, with green eyes. She was always the stable one in their relationship, being well adjusted and self-confident.

They lived together when Zak first got home from the service, but the nightmares and flashbacks started controlling his every thought. He had trouble sleeping and would get up at all hours of the night and replay memories of the war in his head. To try and cope with his issues, he began to drink a little more than he should, and it caused problems between him and Julie when it put a strain on their marriage.

After trying to understand what had happened to him, Julie realized he needed help she couldn't give him. He would raise his voice at her and sometimes go into temporary temper rages, and it was a little more than Julie could handle. One day she sat him down and told him she couldn't deal with his PTSD issues and believed they needed to take a break from each other. She told him she still loved him, but she thought he needed to come to terms with his demons and figure things out on his own before they could ever fix things between them and be together again. She suggested a marriage counselor, but Zak wasn't ready.

When he was in the military, he became a member of the elite Special Forces and had many firefights with the enemy during his deployment in Afghanistan. He'd seen more than his fair share of death and destruction during his two tours of duty, and it had changed him forever. Before he had gotten home, he had gone to the military psychiatrists and tried to get help to figure things out, but it was like putting Band-Aids on a fresh wound. Nothing he did ever helped him forget or deal with his issues.

He was 26 years old and still in good physical shape standing six feet one inch tall and weighing 185 pounds, with brown eyes and hair. Not wanting to go to college after his stint with the military, he was happy to land the new job with the forestry department. He'd hoped that would allow him to be out in the open woods and not cooped up in a building somewhere and doing a desk job he hated. He was hoping it would give him some peace of mind because he always loved being in the forest's open air. Most of all, he was hoping the job would help him with his marriage to Julie. He'd already found out that drinking too much alcohol wasn't the way to solve his problems. It only made things worse between the two of them. He also knew he couldn't jeopardize his new job by drinking too much.

He was raised in the small community of Lilliwaup, the nearest town to the Mount Skokomish Wilderness in the northeastern part of the Olympic National Forest. That part of the forest was known as a wild and natural area, and it encompassed 13,278 acres of thick wilderness. One area of Mount Skokomish was known as Sawtooth Ridge, and it's where rock climbers would come from all over to hike and go climbing.

His cousin Seth also worked for the forest department. He was responsible for Zak getting the job when an opening became available at the Forestry Department. He and Zak had lived in Lilliwaup their entire lives, and they knew the Skokomish Wilderness as well as anyone from those parts, maybe even better. He and Seth were about the same age, height, and build and had hung out together since they were youngsters. They spent so much time together growing up they were almost like brothers, and many strangers thought they were. However, he didn't join the military like Zak and chose to stay home and work while Zak was in the Army.

At an early age, he and Zak would pack a sack lunch, and at the break of dawn on Saturdays, they'd be gone until dark, just exploring the wilderness. They pretended that one of them was a good guy and the other one was a bad guy as they played their games in the forest. They loved the backcountry and were remarkably familiar with the two trails that took a person deep into the mountains' dark places. But they used the faint Mildred Lakes Trail the most. They never saw anything that wasn't within the forest's norm, but it always kept them intrigued. They had seen mountain lions and bears but never anything out of the ordinary. They'd heard stories of UFOs and Bigfoot creatures being seen in the woods since they were kids but never saw any themselves. Zak's Grandfather had told stories about seeing them, so he believed they were real.

Seth had never married and lived alone in his little two-bedroom house between Lilliwaup and Hoodsport's towns. His best friend while Zak was gone was his half wolf and half German Shepard dog named Rex. He took Rex with him everywhere he went, and he'd ride and wait for Seth in the back of his four by four Ford pick-up. Rex was five years old and weighed a little over a hundred pounds. His coat was dense, light tan with black around his head and legs. He was a remarkable specimen that was much taller and bigger than the average German Shepard.

Seth had gotten Rex as a gift from his Indian friend, Walker, when he was just a puppy. Even then, he was sensitive and had remarkable hearing abilities. Seth would put him in another room of the house and then whisper his name, and Rex could hear it. He had sharp eyes that didn't miss anything, but he didn't do well around loud noises, new people, and fast motion. He became strongly attached to Seth and was very playful with him. Because of the strong wolf prey drive, he didn't like animals like rabbits, cats, and hamsters. He just saw them as food, so Seth had to keep him away from them.

Seth found at an early age that Rex was energetic and would become destructive to things in the house when he left him alone for several hours. No matter how much he trained him, Rex remained destructive when left alone that long. Sometimes Seth didn't know if he could trust him around other people because he would growl and show his teeth when someone he didn't know came around. Because Zak was around a lot when Seth first got him, Rex was comfortable around him and trusted him as well.

He tore everything up in the house, so Seth built a sizeable fenced-in area in his back yard to keep Rex while he was at work. It was eight-foot-high above the ground and two feet below the ground. He made it large enough so that it gave Rex plenty of exercise area and lots of shade. He had a nice large doghouse that Rex used to get out of the bad weather when it rained or snowed. He always did when he got home from work to let Rex in the house and started petting and playing with him. Seth kept his freezer full of elk that he fed to Rex along with a chicken now and then because he needed a diet high in protein. He would occasionally throw him a good size bone so he would get the calcium he needed.

When Seth started training Rex, it took a tremendous amount of patience because he kept getting sidetracked with his natural wild instincts. Rex had to establish the Alpha position to get Rex to respond well to him, but they loved each other, and as he got older, Rex always wanted to please his master.

While Zak was in the Military, Seth spent a great deal of time fishing and hunting at his favorite places in the forest and nearby lakes and rivers. He also spent a lot of time at Sawtooth Ridge, where rock climbers liked to spend their day climbing to the top. Seth became an avid rock climber and loved to climb the Ridge every chance he got. He always left Rex home when he went climbing because he knew it would be no fun for him to sit for hours in the back of the truck just waiting for him.

On his next day off, Zak was busy with something, so Seth decided to climb up at the ridge. During the climb, he was all alone and about halfway up his climb when he stopped for a moment to rest and take in the scenic view. As he hung there on the side of the mountain, he stared out over the vast, wide-open space when suddenly he spotted something that would forever change his life. At first, he thought it was some military airplane that was fast approaching his location. As it got closer to where he was perched, he realized it wasn't an airplane at all, it didn't have any wings, and it was round. It didn't pay any attention to him as he watched in disbelief as the strange object flew within fifty yards of him. It was like nothing he's ever seen before, except in science fiction movies.

He squinted and blinked his eyes a few times to make sure that what he saw was real and not a figment of his imagination. He'd seen lights in the sky before, but it was always at night and not in the daylight hours. It was a bright shining disc type of craft, and it illuminated such brightness Seth couldn't look directly at it without it hurting his eyes. The rays of sun bounced off the craft in a thousand different directions. It flew past him as if he weren't there and to the base of the ridge when it instantly came to an abrupt halt in mid-air. It was right below him as it moved into a hovering position. It just made a slight humming sound as it sat there suspended in midair.

Seth believed it might be some government drone because of its lightning speed, no wings, and sound. Stunned, he sat there and observed the craft as he thought, "What the hell is this thing? That's amazing." It sat and hovered about fifteen feet off the ground. Within a few minutes, a door opened on the bottom of the craft, and a light shined toward the ground. To Seth's astonishment, two massive creatures slowly ascended and were gently lowered through the light to the ground. Seth couldn't believe his eyes as he sat there in total shock and disbelief and watched, not quite registering what he was seeing. The creatures' size and shape were bigger than any bear he'd ever seen before, but they resembled a bear in some ways. They were hairy all over their body with thick brown hair and were very muscular. Although they had a slightly protruding snout, they looked and walked upright, like a human. Seth shook his head a couple of times to see if he had some type of illusion or if his eyes were deceiving him.

To his utter amazement, the craft left the two creatures on the ground, and as suddenly as it had appeared, it darted into the sky at supersonic speed and disappeared. Seth kept his eyes glued to the craft for several seconds until it was out of sight and then turned his attention back toward the creatures. He whispered in astonishment, "What the hell was that and what are those creatures they left behind!" He watched as the creatures hesitated and seemed to get their bearings and then started making their way up the canyon until they disappeared into the woods. Once they disappeared, he sat there for several minutes to slow his heart rate down and try to compose himself. He was no longer interested in getting to the top of the Ridge. It took him a while to get down off the mountain, and he was thinking, "what the hell was that? I need to tell Zak about what I saw, but what if he doesn't believe me? If he doesn't believe me, then I can't tell anyone about this. Nobody else will ever believe me; they'll think I'm just plain crazy."

When he got home, he pulled off all his gear and sat down on the sofa next to Rex. He put his hand on Rex's shoulders and said, "Boy, you're not going to believe what I saw today. I'm not even sure I believe what I saw myself. If I hadn't seen it with my own two eyes, I'd probably think I dreamed or imagined it." Rex looked up and wagged his tail. Seth continued, "It was the craziest damn thing I've ever seen in my life." He then went on to tell Rex all about the entire encounter. At least Rex listened and didn't think he was crazy.

For the next several nights, what he'd seen was haunting him, and he was having a hard time sleeping. All kinds of thoughts and ideas were going through his head as he questioned if he should even tell Zak. He was wondering what those creatures were and why the spaceship had dropped them off in the forest. All his life, he'd heard stories about UFOs, Sasquatch, or Bigfoot and wanted to see them but never did until now. He wondered if the creatures were friendly, like what he'd heard people say about the indigenous Bigfoot creatures they had encountered in the past? It was the unknown that began to haunt him, and his thoughts were starting to drive him crazy. He was beginning to doubt himself and what he saw as he said, "Maybe I temporarily blacked out, maybe it didn't happen at all?"

For the next several weekends, he turned down invitations to do things with Zak and his friends because he didn't want to tell anyone about his encounter. He just wanted to go back up to Sawtooth Ridge on the weekends and climb up to the same spot and wait and see if the UFO or the creatures would return. After doing that a few weekends and not seeing any sign of them, it started to get under his skin. He became distant with friends and people he worked with until finally, one day Zak, knowing something was wrong, asked him what was going on with him.

He was reluctant to talk about anything at first but knew he couldn't continue to carry the burden of what he'd seen inside. He told Zak, "I've got something I need to talk to you about when we get a chance, but not right now."

Zak said, "Ok, just let me know when you're ready." Zak wondered what it was that was bugging him, but he gave him his space. Seth decided he had to sit down with Zak and tell him all about the encounter. He knew Zak would at least listen to him and not make fun of or ridicule him about his wild UFO and creatures' story.

He had Zak meet him at Bessie's restaurant the following morning, and he picked a secluded table in the corner of the room. Once they sat down, he looked around to make sure no one listened to their conversation before he began to speak.

Zak said, "Man, you are acting weird. Is everything ok with you?" His voice wasn't much more than a whisper as he carefully chose his words and told Zak all about the UFO and the two creatures he'd seen come out of the craft.

When he finished, Zak laughed aloud because he thought the whole thing was a joke, as he said, "Ok, you got me; you're pulling my leg, right." Seth sat back up straight in his chair and crossed his arms with a stoic stern look on his face. He didn't laugh or even smile as Zak tried to make light of what he'd told him and tried to get him to admit it wasn't true. But Zak had seen that look several times before when they were younger and realized that Seth was dead serious about what he was telling him.

After sitting there silent for a minute or two, he asked Seth to tell him the entire story again from the beginning. He was now paying careful attention to every word Seth had to say. Even though he'd first been skeptical about the story, he was now intrigued and wanted Seth to tell him every detail about his encounter. Mesmerized by it, Zak was sitting there wide-eyed when he finally asked, "So, what did those damn things look like, exactly?"

Seth thought for a minute as he paused and said, "I know this may sound crazy, but they looked like the pictures we've all seen on television of Bigfoot, only a lot more massive and muscular with a small snout like a grizzly bear. From where I was watching them from above, one of them appeared to be a male about eight-foot-tall with extremely broad shoulders. The other one was smaller, and I believed it to be a female, and it was about seven feet tall and a little less thick and broad than the larger one. They both had long dark brown hair all over their bodies, except for their faces. I could see their eyes, nose, and face clear from where I was sitting.

Zak said, "You do realize that a Bigfoot has never been captured, dead or alive, anywhere on this earth? There's a lot of circumstantial evidence from hundreds of eyewitness accounts, footprints, hair samples, and fuzzy pictures, but no real evidence of the huge creature, hell, a lot of the stories come from right up here in our forest,"

Seth replied, "After I saw those creatures come out of the UFO that day, it makes me think that maybe they are some Alien race and not a known creature of this earth. Maybe that's why no one has ever found physical proof that they exist. Maybe they are being picked up by other aliens in their UFOs when they come in close contact or are shot by humans or maybe whenever they die. From most reports, it seems like every time they do encounter humans, they disappear. Who knows Zak? Maybe they're also the ones connected to the hundreds of missing people reports all over the world? Maybe they are the ones taking them?"

Zak said, "Man, you've been giving this a lot of thought, I can tell! Who knows, maybe anything is possible after what you saw. It sounds like you had a once-in-a-lifetime encounter, but no one will ever believe you. We'll have to keep this our secret for now."

We need to search for the creatures ourselves on our days off work and see if we can find out where they are hiding and take a few pictures of them. If we can get the photos, then we will have proof that they are out there, and then we can show them to the Sheriff and the town people to back up your story."

They talked about his sighting for some time and agreed not to tell anyone about the encounter until they had more proof of what he had seen.

Chapter 2 - The War

Zak returned home to Lilliwaup from the horrors of the war in Afghanistan and thought he could resume the everyday life he had before the military and start the process of healing. Unfortunately, he was having difficulty dealing with some of his experiences and just trying his best to forget them. The only person he had ever tried to talk to about his experiences was Julie, but he didn't do a very good job of that. He couldn't tell her everything that took place during his tours of duty. He believed she'd have a hard time grasping the horrible reality of what he went through. Not being honest about his experiences, coupled with his PTSD issues, drove a wedge between the two of them. Foolishly, he didn't think she would've been able to deal with the things he'd seen and done while he was in the military.

During one of their recent fishing trips, Seth began to question Zak about everything he'd gone through while in Afghanistan. He told Zak that ever since he'd joined the military and gotten home, he'd changed and was now more like a loner than his best friend. After giving it some thought, Zak decided to tell Seth all about his experiences. He was reluctant to talk about some of the hurtful things at first, but he began to tell Seth everything after some coaxing.

He began by telling Seth he was a member of the Alfa Company of the Stingray Brigade, based out of Tacoma, Washington. "We were stationed near the Hindu Kush Mountain Range that reached heights up to 24,580 feet at the highest point. When we arrived, we were told that we were being sent to Afghanistan to track down the elusive Taliban soldiers. The problem with that is, once there, you couldn't tell the difference between local nationals and enemy soldiers. They all looked and acted the same. You never knew who the enemy was unless they were shooting at you. During my first three months in Afghanistan, the Taliban were able to evade every patrol we sent out, so we never engaged the enemy. I figured that was a good thing because none of our men were being ambushed, wounded, or killed. We believed in what the Army was telling us that we were supposed to win hearts and minds by protecting the Afghan people's general population.

I was on my second tour in Afghanistan when I grew bored with minimal enemy contact, so I asked the Commander to give me a different duty assignment. I told him about my experience of being in the mountains here in the Northeastern Skokomish Wilderness in Washington and that I had been out in the elements during rain and snow many times. It took a few days, but he called me into his office and offered me a new assignment that nobody else wanted."

He said, "I was going to be given a duty of hunting down one of the most notorious and ruthless serial killers to ever come out of Afghanistan. His name was Abdullah Shief, and it was estimated he'd killed over 30 American and NATO soldiers and over 30 other innocent people from various villages stretching from Kabul to Jalalabad. He had even killed one of his wives, and his nickname given to him by his enemies was "The Wild Dog." It was believed he was hiding deep in the mountains somewhere between the Hindu Kush and the Pamir Mountains. My job was to hunt him down and kill him.

Shief was around 36 years old and portrayed as a sociopath, a crazed killer, with pure hatred for Americans, NATO allies, and many Afghans. He was feared by those that were around him and knew him. He was a crazy killer and a true monster. His favorite way to kill his victims was to take them to a high point on one of the mountains and tie their hands behind their backs. Then he would tie a long elastic strip taken from American gunships or helicopters to a tree or large rock and then wrap it around their legs. While they were still alive, he would then push them off the mountain. The fall was planned out so that it was just enough to where their heads and upper body would hit the ground, and then their crushed bodies would spring back up in the sky, much like a bungee jumper, but with a different result. He took particular delight in watching the crushed body spring back up in the air as he laughed aloud and danced while the body just dangled in the air. I went out alone into enemy territory and learned to survive in extremely harsh conditions, just searching for the monster. A few times, I was so cold out in the elements I thought I would freeze to death. I would get information from local villagers about where Shief was hiding because they wanted him dead just as much as the United States Military. I also got my food and water from them while I stayed hidden during my search.

Several times I trailed him from the mountains of Hindu Kush to the caves of Tora Bora and almost had him on numerous occasions. He knew the mountainous area well and was intelligent and elusive, so he would go into hiding when he knew that I was close to him. There were times when some of the Afghans that were sympathetic to the Taliban and Shief would try to ambush me and kill me. I managed to avoid being shot and killed, and in return, I killed a lot of them that came after me. I had people hunting me while, at the same time, I was pursuing him. A few times, I had genuine fear they would kill me, but I somehow made it out alive. It had become a matter of kill or be killed as I hunted for him.

After several months of living from place to place and fending for myself, I finally trapped him in an area of the steep mountains of Hindu Kush. I called the commander and gave him his location, and they sent in an airstrike and bombed the area repeatedly until everything was flattened. I was told to return to the base camp after the locals told our commanders that Shief had been killed. My goal of hunting for that monster was over, and I had accomplished my mission. I chose to be in the right place at the right time, and that's why my Army buddies started calling me the "Monster Hunter."

It was then that I realized there are real monsters in this world, but God is greater, and a force of goodwill always triumphs. We don't always choose those paths, but inherently it moves us forward and guides our lives, and shows us our true nature. That's when we realize our path was laid out when we were young; we can be a force of good. Big or small, our actions define us, and I know I'm a force of good."

Seth listened to Zak's story and said, "Man, that is some crazy-ass stuff. Thanks for telling me. I have always wondered what you went through over there. You have to tell Julie everything you just told me. You don't need to keep all of that from her. She's an intelligent girl and needs to know." Zak promised he would talk to her about it as soon as he felt the time was right.

Chapter 3 - The Forest

According to many Bigfoot enthusiasts, the Pacific Northwest forests in Washington are where many of the Bigfoot population live. They claim there have been over 600 sightings of Bigfoots by people in the state of Washington alone. Zak and Seth always believed that part of Washington had all the qualities the Bigfoots needs to thrive in the wilderness. It has high forest cover density, proximity to freshwater sources, proximity to roads, caves, a large concentration of mule deer, and it's not significantly populated by humans. It's the perfect cover for wildlife and Bigfoots.

The location of Seth's sighting of the UFO and the creatures was at the base of Sawtooth Ridge, where there's a lot of old-growth with western hemlock, western red cedar, and Douglas fir trees that dominate the area. Once the alien craft dropped off the creatures, they headed to the higher elevation toward the firs, pines, and dwarf junipers. In the higher elevation, there are known caves, and Seth believed that was the creature's destination.

The lower valley areas are home to nine American Indian Tribes with 33 settlements and 730 people. One of the tribes is the Skokomish Indians (meaning big river people). Zak and Seth had become friends with one of the members of the tribe over the years that called himself Walker, although his Indian name was "Little Fish." He once told them about his people seeing lights in the sky for years, throughout the mountains and forest, and understanding and trust in the Sasquatch. Over the years, he told Zak and Seth, the Indians have lived in harmony with them for centuries and never had any trouble with them. They never paid too much attention to Walker's stories until now, and they were coming back to them. They were going to locate Walker and find out what he might know about the creatures Seth had seen dropped out of the craft.

Seth talked to Walker, and they agreed to meet up with him the following Saturday. They were going to take Mildred Trail to get to Walker's village, and if they left about six in the morning, they could be there by mid-morning. Zak was excited to go check things out as he thought, "Maybe we can spot one of the creatures along the way and get a picture of them." He knew it was against the law to kill a Bigfoot in Washington, but they were going to have their weapons with them for protection against bears and mountain lions.

As they left that morning, it had already been about three weeks since Seth had his encounter at the Ridge. Rex was by his side as they took the trail and headed for the Elwha Indian Reservation village. They were very observant as they went deeper into the woods, but it was an uneventful three-hour hike through the dense forest before they made it to Walker's Village. When they first got there, Rex heard the other dogs barking in the village and barked back at some of them, and it alerted the tribe. It was only a few minutes when several armed Indians soon met up with them on the edge of the village. Seth had his hand on Rex's shoulders as he growled at them, and Seth said, "It's an ok boy."

Seth quickly introduced himself and Zak to the Indians and told them they were friends of "Little Fish." When he said that, one of the Indians got Walker and brought him to meet up with them. When he got there, they exchanged greeting, and Seth asked him if they could talk to him about something he'd seen in the forest. He could tell Zak and Seth were serious, so he took them to an area where they could sit and talk for a while. A couple of the other Indians tagged along because they were curious about what they had to say.

Walker said, "Man, that Rex sure turned into a beautiful dog."

Seth smiled and replied, "Yep, he's a good boy, and my buddy, thanks for giving him to me." He reached down and proudly stroked Rex's head.

Rex sat next to Seth as he began to tell Walker all about his encounter with the UFO and the creatures, "I witnessed a strange thing while I was rock climbing up on Sawtooth Ridge about three weeks ago, and I wanted to talk to you about it." He told Walker the entire story about what he'd seen, and when he was finished, he said, "I remember you telling us stories about sightings your tribe has had in this area for hundreds of years regarding the Sasquatch. We wanted to know if your people have seen the two creatures around here that I saw come out of the UFO?"

Walker was wide-eyed, and he seemed a little agitated as his voice raised when he started telling Zak and Seth his people have talked about the sky people that had come down to earth for many years. He said, "It's been passed down for generations about the star people riding in flying craft in the sky. Up there in the mountains' caves, our people have made carvings, symbols, and hieroglyphs of a craft and a creature that was a half-human and half-animal that we call Sasquatch. My people believe we still have contact with beings from far away realms and dimensions. Most of us have seen the flying objects and Sasquatch with our own eyes. The Sasquatch and our tribe have lived in harmony with each other and have never been attacked by them. The Sasquatch has their language, and you can hear them in the forest at night, calling to each other. They growl, snort, snarl, whistle, and scream, and our elders believe they know what every sound they make means, and we've never lived in fear of them. Our people hold all of this information as sacred."

His voice deepened as he said, "I will tell you guys something, but you have to make me a promise that you won't share it with the Sheriff or any people in town. We don't want a lot of people disturbing our peaceful way of life."

They quickly replied, "You can trust us, Walker. We won't share anything you say with anyone."

Walker continued, "As I said, we've had a peaceful co-existence with the sky people and the sasquatch for many years until last week. We thought we could live with the belief that the sasquatch adhered to some moral code that we've lived by for centuries. But that all changed during the middle of the night when two creatures resembling a Sasquatch came into our village. They took a six-year-old girl and one of our elders. They were different than the Sasquatch we've seen in the past. Those two were not peaceful and kind like the others; they were more like monsters, just wanting to cause harm to the people of our village.

After the little girl and the elder were taken, we put together a search party, and early the following day, we started tracking the animals. We followed them to the caves up in the mountains, and there is one of the caves where we found the body of our elder. The flesh had been ripped and torn from his body as if he'd been eaten. There was no sign of the girl. We wrapped up what was left of the body and got it ready to take back to our village. Once that was done, we continued to follow the animals' tracks to a higher elevation in the mountains until we felt like it was getting too steep and treacherous to continue with a large group.

That's when we heard the crying of the girl, and she was in an area that was almost impossible to get to by foot, but after a steep climb, we were able to reach her, save her, and bring her down. Everyone was surprised when we found that the animals didn't harm her. There was no physical damage that was done to her at all by the animals. We went back and got the remains of our elders and took them to our village. Our people have always believed that all entities are good or bad, inherently like a bear confronting a human face to face and then releasing them unharmed. That must have been what happened with the little girl.

We didn't tell the townspeople what had happened for fear they would have the Sheriff and other people all over our village. They would have their guns and trying to hunt the animals down and kill them. Some of the elders of our tribe believe we must have offended the star people and the Sasquatch, and that's why they came into our village and took the little girl and killed the elder. Letting the girl go was just a warning to our tribe that they could do it anytime they want if we don't change our way."

Zak and Seth thanked him for the information and promised to keep Walker's secret to themselves before they left. Seth told Walker they were going to start searching for the animals to get proof they were in the woods.

They had to get back home before it got too late because they didn't want to be out with those two creatures at night. On the way back, Zak said, "That was a bizarre story, but now, more than ever, I'm starting to think those stories about vanishing people in the forests and parks may have something to do with these creatures. Some of the stories of missing people sound eerily similar. We also now know they are killers, and they will eat human flesh. Weirdly, the villagers think they may have offended the Star people and the Sasquatch in some way."

Chapter 4 - The First Hunt

It was about a week later, and Seth got a phone call from Walker, and he told him he had one of his Indian friends by the name of Ben Samuels that wanted to meet with him and Zak. He said he wanted to be their guide when they searched for the creatures. Seth made plans for Ben to meet up with him and Zak the following Saturday at the beginning of the Mildred Trail at the edge of the forest. Walker told him he would have Ben there on Saturday morning at 6:00.

When they arrived on Saturday, Ben was already waiting for them as Rex growled at him. Seth said, "It's ok, boy; he's our friend." After that, Rex was ok with Ben. He was in his mid-sixties and had his hair pulled back into a ponytail. He had gray around his temples and carried an old smooth walking stick and a rifle strapped over his left shoulder. He was a quiet man but introduced himself and told Zak and Seth, and he was happy to go with them to hunt down the creatures.

Zak told him they were happy to have him as their guide and welcomed his company and extra gun. They had their rifles over their shoulders and pistols in their belts as they started their hunt through the forest.

Zak asked Ben why he was willing to help them find the creatures, and he said, "The man the creatures took from our village was my brother. When they came into our village and took my brother, it was the first time we've ever had problems with any of the Sasquatch. I think these creatures are different from those we've known in the past, and they have a thirst to kill. If we find these two, we need to kill them. They are evil and not friends with our people or anyone else. They look and act like they are some mixed breed of the Sasquatch, but they are highly intelligent. They knew just the right time at night to take my brother and the little girl without any resistance."

Zak said, "I'm sorry about you losing your brother. If we find the creatures, we'll let you kill them yourself." He shook his head up and down in agreement and didn't say anything else. He figured if Ben killed one of them, nobody would ever find out he killed a Sasquatch.

As they made their way deep into the forest, Ben pointed out a strange tree that had been bent into a complete arch. It looked as though it was a total manipulation of the tree and not normal. Two logs braced the top to form a triangle. All around the tree and in a circle were fallen broken tree limbs. Ben said, "Sasquatch did this. You can tell because it's done with some intelligence. After all, they are brilliant." Rex was busy sniffing all around the area as they talked. "They use these trees for navigating and as territorial markings. I believe it helps them find their way back to their hiding places, and they have several of them. We need to keep an eye out for these types of signs."

At one point, Ben spotted a grouping of smaller trees that all had been bent together, and it looked a little like a crude Indian teepee. Ben said it was made so the creatures could crawl into them and hide or rest. He said, "This is one of their nests; they also have them throughout the forest." Zak and Seth had seen things like them before but didn't know what they were. They just thought the bears had something to do with them.

While they continued upward toward the cave area, Zak asked Ben if he'd seen the UFOs in the sky himself before. Ben said, "I've lived here all my life, and the forest is all I know, so yes, I've seen the UFOs many times. They maneuver their flying machines in the woods over the mountains with their lights shining like a beacon in the night sky. They've been coming and going from our forests for many years. I've even had close encounters with some of the Sasquatch myself. They've always been friendly and not evil like these two creatures they left behind this last time. Even though our elders believe we may have offended them, our village is now protecting ourselves against these creatures for the first time just in case they come back again."

They stopped several times along the way and just listened to see if they could hear the calls or other noises from the creatures. A few times, Rex would stop, bristle and growl. By midday, they had made it to the first cave that was hidden up high in the side of the mountains when Zak asked, "So Ben, have you seen or heard anything that sounds or looks like it might be the creatures since we've been searching today?"

Ben replied, "I've seen shadows far out in the distance, and they've been watching us for a few miles now, but they're masters at staying hidden. They won't be seen unless they want us to see them. They're stalking us right now, so I'm hoping they'll come out in the open so we can get a shot at them."

When they got to the cave opening, Zak and Seth got out their flashlights, took the rifles off their shoulders, and had them ready just if they had an encounter with some wild animal or one of the creatures. The three of them and Rex cautiously headed into the cave, searching every step they took. They walked deeper into the cave until they came to what Ben called a nest, and Rex let out a light bark as they got close to it. It was a rounded-out area of the cave wall, and it had branches and other foliage on the floor of the crude bed. Ben told them he believed it was where the creatures had been spending some of their time, but it wasn't their permanent location.

When they left the cave, Ben said, "We need to head back home because with these evil creatures roaming the woods, we don't want to be out here too long after dark. When we get down a little lower, I'll split up from you guys and head back to my village."

Rex had been out in the forest hundreds of times with Seth, but this was only the second time since the creatures arrived. Seth and Zak had decided to take Rex with them every time they went into the woods to hunt for the creatures because he could alert them when the creatures were near. They knew he would be able to hear or see the creatures before they could. Rex didn't know what they were searching for but loved being out in the woods with the guys. Seth kept him close to him most of the time and didn't let him stray too far away and take off chasing deer, elk, or some other varmint.

As they made it a little further down the trail, Rex stopped suddenly and looked back in the cave entrance direction. The hair on the back of his neck bristled, and he growled aloud. Seth said, "Hey, what's the matter, boy, what do you see?" Rex looked up at Seth, wagged his tail, and then looked back toward the thick tree line and growled again. This time it was deeper and a more threatening growl. Seth said, "There's something out there that he sees. It's probably them."

Ben said, "Yep, he must've spotted the creatures out there. Something sure caught his attention. I've been having an uncomfortable feeling for about thirty minutes that something has been following us up to the caves. Now on the way back. I couldn't see what it was, but it is hiding just inside the tree line. It might be the creatures we've been looking for, so be alert and keep your eyes open." It was just about that time they heard the creature's chattering back and forth to each other on the edge of the woods. Zak told Seth and Ben to get ready as they each gripped their rifles with both hands in case of an attack.

They had gone only about another quarter of a mile further down the trail, and the brush and trees had gotten thicker when suddenly the male creature jumped out from behind a large grouping of bushes and trees and tried to grab Seth. Seth saw him out of the corner of his eye and immediately ducked back as the creature just missed in its attempt to take him. As soon as the creature did that, Rex started fighting with it, and he was biting at his legs and swinging arms as it retreated into the woods. Being temporarily distracted by Rex, it gave up on trying to get Seth. Zak took a wild shot at the creature, but he was already in the dense woods and blocked from a clear shot.

Zak yelled to Seth, "Did you see that son of a bitch; he almost got you?" Seth was busy with his attention, now focused on Rex as he yelled for him to come back. Rex wasn't going to give up easily because the creature was trying to get his master, and he wasn't having any part of it. He followed the creature a little deeper into the woods and was already a few hundred yards away, barking and biting at the creature when the guys heard the curdling death yelps of Rex. Within a few seconds, everything went silent.

Seth said, "Oh, no. That bastard got Rex! We have to get to him quick!" He feared the worst as they took off in the direction where they'd heard the yelps. It took them several minutes to find Rex's lifeless and mangled body, and by the time they got there, he was lying motionless and wasn't breathing. It looked as though the creature killed Rex with a few strong blows to the neck and head. Rex still had a large amount of the creature's hair in his clenched teeth.

Seth fell to his knees and broke down and cried out, "That son of a bitch killed Rex, he died trying to protect me." He stood up and started kicking the ground and anything that was in his path as he let out his anger. Zak and Ben were scanning the area to see if the creature was still around, but it was gone. Once he was able to collect himself, Seth said, "I'm going to kill that fucker now, no more being a nice guy for me. If it's ok with you guys, I would like to carry Rex's body back home and bury him in the backyard."

Zak replied, "Sure, no problem, I'll help you carry him and help you bury him when we get back. I'm sorry Seth, I loved that guy too. He was a good companion and a great friend, and we're going to miss him." Seth had tears in his eyes as they picked up Rex's body and continued down the trail, looking back for the creatures as they went.

On the way back, Zak said, "I stuck that hair that was in Rex's mouth in a plastic bag, and we'll take it to a lab within the next week or so and have a DNA test done on it. Rex is going to make it possible for us to find out for sure what kind of creature these monsters are."

Once they were in the lower part of the wilderness, Ben said, "Ok, this is where I leave you, boys. I'm sorry about your dog Seth. He was a faithful friend and companion."

Seth was a little despondent as he said in a soft, sad voice, "Thank you, Ben, I appreciate that."

Zak said, "Give us a call Ben, you can join us any time you want. We're going to keep coming out until we get those bastards."

That's when Seth said to Zak, "It's personal now, Zak, they killed my best friend. I'm going to try my best to kill them if I see one of them again. I'm not going to try and prove that they are out there anymore."

Zak didn't blame him; he was feeling the same way as he replied. "I'm with you there, Seth, but you're lucky that creature didn't get its claws in you. If it could've gotten a hold of you, that might be you lying here in my arms instead of Rex."

Seth said, "Those creatures are vicious and evil, and they showed us they have little fear of humans. We have to get rid of them; we have to kill them."

Chapter 5 - The Fear

Gladys Daniels was finishing washing the evening dishes, standing in front of the kitchen window, and looking out toward the woods. She could see that it was beginning to get dark, and her husband Don was relaxing in the living room watching television when Gladys said, "Don, can you go out and grab the mail? I forgot to get it today." Don was getting comfortable after a long day at work and was a little reluctant to move from his cozy chair. As he slowly got to his feet, he mumbled something under his breath, where she couldn't hear him. He grabbed his rifle by the door and headed out.

They lived southeast of Lilliwaup at the edge of the lower portion of the Olympic Forest's high country, and the woods surrounded their property. Their house's driveway to the main road was about two hundred yards down a narrow rock and dirt road and a nice walk to the mailbox and back. All the land around their home was dark, dense forest as far as the eye could see. When the house had originally been built, the parcel had been cleared from the middle of the woods.

They had moved there from Seattle three years earlier to get away from the hustle and bustle of the big city life. Don worked for the city as a new construction inspector, and even though he only had a few more years to work before he retired, the rare opportunity came up for them to purchase the ten-acre farm and transfer with his work. Their kids were grown and married, so it was just the two of them. Even though it was a long way away from their kids, they enjoyed raising chickens, cows, and a few other animals. The property was completely fenced and cross-fenced, where wild animals would have a hard time getting to them.

By the time Don made it to the mailbox, it was already starting to get a little darker. For some reason, he had a funny feeling, like someone was watching him, as the hair stood up on the back of his neck, and he thought, "I better get back pretty soon, it's getting dark out here, and something could sneak up on me before I knew it, then I'd be screwed."

After he'd gotten the mail and started walking back, he glanced down at the mail and then looked back in the direction of the house. He was taking a little off guard when he saw what he thought was a person standing at the end of the driveway and near the house. As he walked toward the house, he kept an eye on the person, standing there and not moving. He had one shoulder lowered as he looked back over his right shoulder toward Don, and he looked as though he was waiting for him to make it back to the house. It was just dark enough that Don couldn't make out the person or his size, though he looked like a big guy. He wondered how the man had gotten there because he knew he didn't see him on the way to get the mail. Don whispered, "Maybe he's been hiding in the barn? That's a chilling thought," He suddenly had an eerie feeling because he now believed the person had been there for a while just watching them. Then Don thought, "Maybe he jumped the fence and came out of the woods." Even so, he was feeling uncomfortable about him being there. He readied his rifle just in case of a confrontation.

He was feeling angry because he felt a little violated that this person was within their fenced-in property. He felt the blood rush from his body up to his face, and he became flushed as he called out to him as he got closer, "Hey there, can I help you?" Nothing, no movement, voice, or anything, as he just stood there looking back at

Don. The fact that he didn't answer back made Don even more angry and apprehensive as he said again. Getting a little closer, he said again, "Hey buddy, can I help you?" Still nothing from the person, so now he was starting to get pissed off the guy wouldn't answer.

As Don got even closer, though it was dark, he realized it wasn't a man at all; it was some human-looking creature that just looked and walked upright like a man. However, it was covered in hair all over its body except for its face. It was a little over eight-foot-tall and massive. Its huge shoulders were twice as broad as a normal size man, and the muscles in his legs and arms were thick and rugged looking. When Don realized it wasn't a man, he started saying, "Oh shit, oh shit, what do I do now. Do I shoot this thing or run for my life back to the house?"

The creature looked ferocious, and it wasn't the least bit afraid of Don, except that Don had the rifle in his hand, and he seemed to be frightened of it. He had it pointed toward the creature and kept his eye glued to it as he slowly crossed between it and the fence that lined the driveway on both sides. He was hoping the creature wouldn't advance on him. He couldn't believe he was within 25 feet of the massive beast, and it hadn't attacked him. As Don passed by, it just continued to stand there the entire time with a motionless and nasty looking scowl in its wrinkled forehead and face.

When Don finally got to the house, he yelled out to Gladys to hurry and take a look at the creature. His voice was raised and excited as he said, "I don't know what the hell that thing is, but it's not a person. It's big and scary looking!" Its head was large and droopy because it didn't look like it had a neck, and its head was constantly looking toward the ground, except when it lifted its head and turned to look at Don once again. He could see the creature's side profile showed a slight muzzle, and he momentarily confused the creature with a bear, but its arms seemed more prolonged than that of a bear.

Just as Gladys and Don stepped out on the porch, the creature turned its attention back toward the house and looked at them as if it wasn't sure if it wanted to attack them or run back into the woods.

When Gladys first saw the creature, the fear instantly engulfed her entire body as she let out a scream and said, "It's a Bigfoot!" When she screamed, the creature let out a high-pitched cry of its own as if it were calling to something or someone and went trotting into the woods. Then Don and Gladys heard a return call from another creature hidden just inside the tree line. Don took a couple of shots over the creature's head as if to scare it away as it headed for the woods. He was hoping the sound of the rifle would be enough to keep the creatures away from their house.

Then the fear set in as they quickly locked all the doors and windows, and Gladys asked Don, "What are we going to do if those creatures come back and try and get us? What if those things come back when you're at work. What if they decide to knock our door down in the middle of the night and come in and kill us both? I'm going to be afraid to go out during the day to feed the chickens and collect the eggs! What about feeding the animals?"

When she said that, Don said, "Ok, let's just calm down a bit, maybe those things just wanted to take one of the young calves, and that's why it didn't come after us." He didn't realize it may be intelligent enough to fear the rifle he was carrying. The reality of seeing the creature now had Gladys in fear for her life. She asked Don again what they would do if the creatures came back while they were sleeping? Don said, "I'll keep my rifle by the bed, and if those things break into the house, then I'll kill them."

That was somewhat comforting, but Gladys had all kinds of thoughts going through her head, "What if Don doesn't have time to shoot them? What if they break through the bedroom windows? What if they decide to rip us limb from limb?" She wasn't going to get much sleep that night.

To try and comfort Gladys, Don said, "Tomorrow morning, I'll talk to Sheriff Philip Kane and see what he says and see what he thinks we should do."

The following day before he left for work, Don went to the Sheriff's office and talked to Sheriff Kane about what they'd seen. Much to Don's surprise, after everything he told the Sheriff, he said, "As long as they aren't trying to hurt you, then you and Gladys should be ok. It was probably just a couple of stray bears."

Don said, "Look, Sheriff, I know what we saw, and they weren't bears. My wife thinks they looked more like a Bigfoot. You have to do something about them because my wife is afraid to come out of the house right now."

To somewhat appease Don, he told him he'd patrol out by that area and keep an eye out for any bears roaming around in the area. Sheriff Kane had already convinced himself that Don and Gladys had just seen and heard a giant bear that was walking upright. However, He could tell that Don's fear was sincere and was afraid of the creatures returning and for their safety.

When Don left his office, the Sheriff mumbled, "Damn city slickers, they always think the worst. After all, it didn't hurt them. What's the big deal?"

Chapter 6 - The Disappearance

Being raised in the Pacific Northwest, Seth had heard and read stories that hundreds of people had vanished from National Parks in the past 100 years. All accounts said that most of the ones that disappeared were young children, two to twelve years old, and the elderly seventy-four to eighty-five years of age. From what he'd learned, fifty percent of the children are found dead, and the ones found alive are located miles away from where they initially disappeared. They were found in areas that seemed impossible for them to get there by themselves. Many of the kids had dogs with them, and the dogs returned, but the children didn't. The ones found alive have refused to talk about their ordeal or say they can't remember what happened. For many of the children's disappearances, the parents said the kids were right behind them as they walked along the trails. However, what is extremely bizarre is that not one older person carrying a firearm has disappeared.

A disappearance is what happened to a local resident, Cecil Shaw, just last weekend. He was five years old. It was just a few days after Don and Gladys saw the creature in their front yard. Since Sherriff Kane didn't tell any of the townspeople about Don and Glady's encounter, the family didn't know and had decided to go on a family picnic outing while taking a hike through the forest. As they were leisurely walking along the main trail in the lower elevation at about 3,500 feet, their son Cecil was scooped up by the giant male creature and whisked away without the family ever knowing what happened. It happened so fast that Cecil didn't even make a sound because the creature immediately placed his large hand over Cecil's mouth and face and ran deep into the woods with him.

When the family turned around to talk to Cecil, they realized he was not right there behind them. They immediately panicked and started searching everywhere for him. They retraced the trail back to the last point where any family members last saw him and nothing. Becoming more frantic, they searched for hours and couldn't find any sign or trace of him. They were devasted, wondering what may have become of him. Did he fall in a hole in the ground, or did a mountain lion or bear grab him without them seeing? They didn't know what happened.

The family later told Sherriff Kane that they were walking along on the trail, and Cecil was right there with them, but he was tagging along in the back. When they turned around, Cecil was gone. They never saw or heard anything that would've alerted them that anything was wrong. At first, they thought he might have fallen into a hole or deep dark crevasse, but they searched the area and nothing — no sign of him anywhere.

Sherriff Kane said, "Yeah, those types of things happen every year. The kids wander off when the parents are preoccupied with something in the forest. That stuff is so thick up there, and if you get off the trail, you could easily get lost." Cecil's family had been in the forest many times and insisted that wasn't what happened. Even though Sheriff Kane had his own opinion of what he thought happened, he went ahead and formed a search party for later that day to go looking for the boy.

When Zak and Seth heard what happened with Cecil, they feared the worst for him, knowing the creatures were out there in the forest. They believed the creatures were the ones that had taken him because they knew what the creatures had done with the little girl from Walker's village. They also knew the creatures had killed the Indian elder and Rex. Now they feared the search party might not find Cecil alive because they knew the creatures had already acquired a taste for human flesh. Although they knew about the creatures, they still couldn't tell anyone about them. They believed it would've started a panic with the townspeople, and a lot of them would've gone out in the woods with guns. Zak figured the woods are so thick they'd be shooting at each other instead of the creatures, or maybe the creatures would get a couple of them too.

Later that day, Zak and Seth armed themselves, joined the party, and searched day and night for Cecil. They combed every square inch of the forest where he disappeared, but there was no sign of him anywhere. Not finding him, they expanded the search to the higher elevation. On the 5th day, Cecil was found at an unbelievable elevation of 6,500 feet in a remote location that the search party had already covered a few times. To everyone's amazement, he was alive and unhurt, except for a few minor cuts and bruises and mild dehydration. Everyone wondered how he got that so high up in the mountain.

Once they had him out of the forest and with his family, Sheriff Kane talked to him and asked what had happened to him during the five days he'd been missing. Cecil was sullen and reluctant to talk about it and said he just stayed with some bears. Relaxing for a minute, Sheriff Kane thought, "I knew it. I knew the bears got him." He asked Cecil what he ate and where he stayed during his ordeal.

He replied, "We ate Huckleberries, and we stayed in a dark cave at night, and the bears kept me warm."

Sheriff Kane now believed the bears had picked him up after he got off the trail and was lost, but he didn't understand why they didn't kill him.

The female creature had recently slightly injured her shoulder in a fall and recuperated from her injury when the male creature abducted Cecil and brought him back to the female. The female creature had a small semblance of a nurturer and mother but only to a small degree. The male brought the child to her to soothe her during her healing time. It was like having a pet to hold and play with. After five days, the female's shoulder was better, so having formed a fondness for him, the creatures decided to let him go. They dropped Cecil off in the upper elevation of the mountain, and it was later that day the search party found him.

Chapter 7 - Secrets

Zak has an older sister named Dera Sanders, who is six years older than him and lives with her husband William and their 7-year-old daughter, Kari. They live in the woods near the small town of Hoodsport, not far away from the place where she and Zak grew up in Lilliwaup. Their home is on five acres and surrounded by the forest. William is a Financial Advisor and travels a lot, doing most of his work out of Seattle. Dera wasn't much afraid of the forest animals, being raised in her entire life, so she was ok with William being gone a lot.

Zak always struggled with trying to keep secrets from his family and especially Dera. However, he'd successfully kept the secrets he carried about his experiences in the war and Afghanistan. Still, now he was having difficulty keeping the secret about the two creatures from her.

Even though he'd never told her anything about his two tours of duty, Dera had heard rumors that Zak was in a few tough combat situations in Afghanistan, but they never talked about them. One time she overheard some of his old war buddies that had visited, speaking, and they joked about calling him the "Monster Hunter."

One evening, while Zak was over for dinner and relaxing at the table, Dera was doing the dishes when Kari went over and sat on the corner of Zak's chair right next to him. She cupped her mouth as she moved in close to his ear and whispered, "I know what you are, Uncle Zak." He was slightly startled as he moved his head backward and looked her right in the face. She cupped her mouth again and moved in close, and whispered, "You're a Monster Hunter." Zak couldn't believe she said that to him and wondered where she'd heard it.

When she said he was a monster hunter, a smile first started to creep onto his face until he remembered why he was given the name monster hunter, and his slight smile then turned into a sad frown.
"Will you help me if a monster ever comes for me?"

As he raised his head, he looked into Kari's little eyes and nodded, "Yes."

Later that evening, Zak thought about what Kari had said to him. After the Indian girl and Cecil Shaw had been abducted and then found high up in the mountains. The creatures killed Benjamin Samuels's brother. It reinforced his feelings about finding the creatures and stopping them from abducting or killing anyone else. He loved his sister and Kari dearly, and concern for their safety was one of the most important things to him. However, he knew he had to keep the secret about the two creatures Seth had seen for now because he didn't want to frighten Kari or Vera.

Zak's grandfather, John Thomas, served in the elite forces called the Marine Corps Raiders in the Marine Corp in WW2. They were the Delta Force of their time. They were disbanded and absorbed into the regular ranks after the war, but they wreaked havoc on the enemy during their time and were feared by them.

That was one reason John settled in the Olympic Forest of Washington state. He wanted to get away from people and crowds after he made it back from the war. He chose to live a quiet life in the mountains to hunt and fish in an unobstructed and unassuming lifestyle.

He'd shared many stories of his military experiences with Zak while on hunting and fishing trips. They went on together. His grandfather was the reason Zak initially enlisted into the military. His grandfather was the one that taught him how to shoot a firearm accurately, how to track animals, and live off the land. Zak not only loved his grandfather but hung on his every word and became his best student throughout the years.

John also had a secret that he never shared with his family until later in life. He, too, had an encounter with what he thought was a Bigfoot creature years before on that same mountain that Seth had encountered. He told Zak the creature he saw was docile and non-threatening, and not dangerous to humans.

He didn't tell any other family members about it because he felt like the creature should be left alone and live its life in the forest, just like he was doing. He came to look at the creature like the Indians did, as peaceful beings and not a threat to anyone. Zak knew the being that his grandfather saw wasn't like the creatures Seth had seen in the mountains because the ones he'd seen were, in the truest sense, monsters.

Chapter 8 - Lab tests on the Creature's Hair

It took Zak and Seth a few weeks to take the same day off during the week so they could go to Belfair, Washington, to submit the hair samples to the lab facility.

Once there, they talked to the researcher, Dr. Nathan Osborn, and his young coworker, Timothy Melrose. At first, they were a little reluctant to tell the two researchers about Seth's encounter, but they seemed eager to see what they thought Zak and Seth had in their possession. Once they handed Dr. Osborn and Timothy the samples, the two men began asking Zak and Seth questions about how they got the samples and what made them decide to bring the samples in so they could be tested. After being questioned about it, Zak spoke up and said, "My cousin Seth here, had a sighting of a UFO and two creatures that were dropped out of the craft by aliens. I happened up there in the mountains of the Olympic Forest."

When he said that, Timothy's eyes widened, and he sat up straight in his chair and leaned forward with intense interest. It was as if he was thinking, "Ok, now we either have two real crackpots on our hands, or these guys believe they saw something." Dr. Osborn started asking Zak and Seth more personal questions about their encounters.

Zak said, "I only saw the creature once and took a shot at him, but Seth saw them on two separate occasions. Once when the aliens dropped the creatures out of the craft, the other time was when the larger creature tried to abduct him in the woods. That was when the creature killed Seth's dog Rex and found the creature's hair in Rex's clenched teeth. We know these creatures are real because we've both seen them. They're not the normal Bigfoot creatures that people have reported seeing in those woods over the years. These are different. These are deadly man-eating creatures."

Timothy very excitedly said, "You got to be kidding me, so you guys were up close to those animals?"

Seth pointed at him and said, "From me to you. That's pretty damn close, too close for comfort. That's when the large creature tried to grab me. I jumped back just before it got me and Zak took a shot at it, then Rex ran after it."

Timothy replied, "Man, that is a close encounter for sure and an amazing story because nobody from around here has ever brought us anything that conclusively proves those creatures are real. Almost every sample we've ever tested came back as bears, wolves, deer, or cows. Now you guys say that you were up close and personal to the animals and have a sample of one of them hair. I excited to see what the tests turn up."

"Yes, that's exactly what we're saying. We haven't told any other people about any of this, and we have no reason to make up this story and go through all this trouble if it wasn't true. We want to know what the hell these monsters are and stop them before they kill anyone else," replied Zak.

Timothy said, "Wait a minute, so you're saying these creatures have killed people?"

Zak replied, "Yes, they went into an Indian village located in the Skokomish Wilderness and abducted a small girl and killed one of the elders of the local Indian tribe. They took him up to the caves and then ate him. They stripped every ounce of flesh from his body."

Timothy let out a gasp and said, "Oh My God, they ate him? That's horrible." "For some reason, we don't know why. They turned the girl free unharmed after five days of captivity." Timothy replied, "That is one of the most bizarre and fascinating stories I've ever heard."

Zak said, "Yeah, well, what about the damn UFO? Don't you think that's a little bizarre too?"

Timothy just shook his head in disbelief and said, "Yes, of course, it is." Zak and Seth didn't think he truly believed that part of the story.

Dr. Osborn could see the men were convinced they saw some Bigfoot animal and a UFO. He said, "We have an entire team of specialists in genetics, forensics, imaging, and pathology, so we'll do our best to find out what type of animals you encountered. However, just so you know, because Rex's saliva is on a lot of the samples, it could compromise the test results."

Dr. Osborn told them he'd seen many test results that had come back negative where people were convinced it was from a Bigfoot, always coming back as nothing more than a bear standing upright. Deep in his heart, he hoped what they had seen was the real thing but believed that what they had seen was just a couple of giant bears. He wasn't sure where the UFO story fit in and if that wasn't just part of Seth's imagination. However, he was willing to test the hair samples to find out what type of bear it might be and put their minds at ease.

Dr. Osborn and Timothy thanked Zak and Seth for bringing in the samples and told them they would get right on it and see what they could find for them. The guys left their contact information but were scratching their heads as they left the lab, wondering if these two experts were really going to test the samples or just going to dismiss everything as a hoax.

As they walked out of the building, Zak said, "You see why I was skeptical about telling people about our encounters. You could tell that Dr. Osborn didn't believe a word we were saying about the creatures. He was being polite and trying to appease us."

Seth replied, "I know, I felt the same way too; it was like we had done something wrong when we first started talking to those idiots. They did act like they started believing us by the time we were getting ready to leave, but who knows?"

Zak replied, "I feel like this was just a wasted trip, and I'll be surprised if we ever hear from them again."

Chapter 9 - Zak tells Julie about the Creatures

Julie was a second-grade teacher at the local grade school, and she'd been busy with schoolwork for the kids and hadn't seen Zak for almost two months. She thought that was a little odd because he checked in on her at least a few times a week. She was beginning to wonder what was going on with him. She missed him and was hoping he'd been working on his PTSD issues.

One of her teacher colleagues suggested that she call Zak and find out what was going on with him. That night when she got home, Julie called, and he answered. She told him she missed him and just wanted to know how he was doing.

Zak knew that eventually, he had to tell Julie about the creatures and tell her about his fears of going into the woods. He wanted to talk to her about them but knew he couldn't do it over the phone. He figured she would think he finally lost his mind and maybe even hang upon him if he told her about them.

He asked her if she would meet him on her day off because he had something confidential and vital to talk to her about things.

She said, "Just tell me now, Zak, I can handle whatever you have to say to me."

He replied, "I can't tell you what we need to talk about over the phone Julie, we need to talk in person about it." At first, she had feared he may be wanting a divorce and asked him if that was why he wanted to talk to her. He said, "God no Julie, nothing like that, I love you, but we must meet and talk about what I want to tell you." She finally agreed to meet him on Saturday at 10:00 am for breakfast at Bessie's restaurant. She knew the suspense of what he had to say was going to drive her crazy for the next few days until they could meet up with each other.

That Saturday morning, Zak got to the restaurant a little early, and he was nervous about telling Julie everything about the creatures as he vigorously rubbed his hands together. He let out a few heavy breaths and sighed a couple of times while waiting for her. He was hoping that once he told her, she didn't just jump up from the table and run out of the restaurant thinking he had lost his mind.

When she got there, she was excited to see Zak as she gave him a big hug and kissed him on the cheek. They took a few minutes and exchanged small talk, and then ordered breakfast. While waiting for their breakfast to come, Julie asked, "So what is so damn important that you wanted to talk to me face to face about and couldn't tell me over the phone? You're driving me crazy!"

Zak replied, "Let's eat our breakfast first, and then I'll tell you everything."

She said, "Oooh! It sounds mysterious.

Zak just raised his eyebrows, smiled, and said, "We'll see."

After they talked through breakfast, Zak nervously said, "I have something I need to tell you, but you have to promise you'll trust and believe in me enough not to think I'm crazy."

She said, "Oh My God! Zak, just tell me what it is!"

He continued, "If you get frustrated and walk out on me, then promise me; you'll talk to Seth about it."

She rolled her eyes and said, "Ok, I promise."

As he started, Zak said, "I'm sure you know that Seth's dog Rex was killed in the woods."

Julie frowned and said, "Yes, I heard about that. That made me sick; he loved that dog so much."

"Well, did you hear that some creature killed it?"

She had a startled look on her face as she replied, "What! No! Are you kidding me? What kind of animal?" Zak studied her every move as he continued to tell her all about Seth's encounter with the UFO and the creatures. He told her about it, killing the local Indian from Walker's tribe and the abduction of the little Indian girl and then finding her alive high in the mountains five days later. He told her he thought that was what had taken Cecil and then turned him loose as well.

She let out a gasp and cupped her hands over her mouth, and quietly said, "I heard the story about the Indian, the little girl, and Cecil, but everyone in town just believed it was a large bear that had killed the Indian elder."

Zak looked her in the eyes and said, "No, it wasn't any bear, it was the two creatures that Seth and I saw, they are killers and Seth, and I have been out every weekend looking for them, that's why you haven't seen or heard from me. I didn't want to scare you. Rex was with me, Seth, and an Indian guide named Ben when we were hunting the creatures up by the caves, and one of the creatures jumped out of the bushes and tried to grab Seth. If Seth hadn't been quick enough, it would've gotten him. Rex fought him off, and I took a shot at the creature, but it was already deep in the thick woods, and I missed. Rex followed it and tried to fight it off, and that's how he was killed."

Julie replied, "Oh My God, Zak, you're serious about all this?"

He lowered his head and said, "I'm dead serious about this, Rex had hair from the creature in his mouth, and we took it to a research center in Belfair, and they're testing it right now. We're just waiting for the results of those tests. Seth and I figure it's some hybrid the aliens created and dropped off here in our woods. We don't know why but they chose our forest to do it."

Julie was in shock and having a hard time believing the story, but she knew Zak wasn't a liar, and he was sincere about everything he'd told her. Julie asked, "So have you told the Sheriff about them."

Zak looked up at her again and said, "No, we wanted to have proof before we told him about the creatures, he has his head buried in the sand and thinks they're just bears."

Julie shivered and said, "Wow. So, what you're telling me is those creatures are out there in the woods, and they're killing and abducting people?"

Zak shook his head up and down and said, "That's what I'm telling you, and I don't want you to go into the woods until we hunt these creatures down and kill them. We need to keep everyone out of those woods that we can."

Julie thought for a minute and then said, "Oh, man. Zak, there's a group of tourists that came in on a bus this morning, and they're hiking up to Sawtooth Ridge and spending the night in the woods and then head back tomorrow. We have to go tell Sheriff Kane what you just told me so he can go out there and warn them."

Zak paid the bill, and they immediately left the restaurant as Julie jumped in Zak's truck, and they headed for the Sheriff's department. When they got there, the receptionist, Judy, told them the Sheriff would be out of the office all day but would be back tomorrow morning. Zak and Julie didn't want to tell Judy about the creatures because they were afraid. She'd spread it all over town and cause a panic with the people in town.

Julie was a matter of fact as she said, "From now on, Zak, I want to go with you and Seth when you hunt for those creatures. I know how to shoot a rifle, and I don't want them killing you, Seth, or any of my friends and family, so I'm going with you." Zak knew better than trying and arguing with her once she'd made up her mind to do something.

Chapter 10 - The Tourists

The bus was packed full of 19 hikers and their gear from the Oceanside Hikers Club out of Seattle. They had planned their trip for several months to the Skokomish Wilderness, where some of them were going to climb to the top of Sawtooth Ridge, while others were going to hike the trails and enjoy the beautiful scenery.

When the bus arrived, it was early in the morning, and the sun's rays were starting to peek through the trees. They enthusiastically unloaded their gear, took in the fresh smell of the pines, and headed up the trail. They were happy to be there as they laughed and talked while trekking along the trail. By mid-morning, they were deep in the forest and oblivious to any dangers, other than a few sore limbs and sore feet.

When they got close to the Ridge, they set up a temporary camp with tents and camping gear where they were going to spend the night. They were going to build a campfire and sit around talking and staring up at the millions of stars in the sky when it got dark.

Everyone was excited they had made the trip, but three anxious climbers were biting at the bit to get on the Ridge and start climbing. They wanted to climb to the top and back before it got dark. They didn't waste any time putting their things away in their tents and leaving the rest of the hikers behind as they headed toward the base of the Mountain. They hadn't even considered taking a rifle or anything else to protect themselves because they had no fear of what may be in the forest.

The three climbers were almost to their destination when they heard the unusual gut-wrenching cry from one of the creatures, and it wasn't too far from them. The sound made them freeze in their tracks as they looked at each other and then looked around to see what could have made that chilling sound. One of them yelled out, "What the hell was that? I've never heard anything like that in the woods before?"

Another wide-eyed climber replied, "I don't know, but it sounded like it was close, big, and creepy."

For the first quarter of a mile, they felt as though they were being stalked by something watching them. The hikers had an uneasy feeling as they could hear breaking branches and the rustling of the leaves just in the thick tree line, not too far away, but whatever it was, it was staying just far enough away that they couldn't see their stalkers. They heard the unusual chatter between the creatures as they made grunting and growling sounds, and the climbers had no idea what it could be. One of the hikers said, "Man, there's something weird out there. It may be a large female grizzly with a couple of cubs. Maybe the cubs are the ones making those strange sounds."

They continued walking toward their destination, but their step had become a little faster as they kept looking in the woods to both sides of the trail to see if the animals were still on their trail. One of the hikers said, "Hey guys, I just saw the shadow of something huge up ahead of us. I couldn't quite make it out, but it might be a large grizzly. We need to turn around and head back to camp while we still can."

One of the climbers replied, "I'm not turning back. You guys go ahead if you want to, but I've been planning this climb for a long time, and I'm not going to let a bear scare me from getting up there."

The other two hikers said, "Ok, you go for it, that may be a female bear with cubs, and if you get too close to them, she could get pretty nasty and aggressive with you, maybe even maul you." He shrugged it off as he said, "I'll meet up with you guys back at the camp," as he turned and started up the trail again. The other two hikers quickly turned around and started back toward camp.

He'd only gotten about thirty yards when the female creature charged him from behind a tree. She knocked him to the ground and began to maul him. He was screaming for his life as the other two climbers heard what happened and turned around to see. They stood there, stunned for a brief second, and watched as the massive creature began to crush their friend with her massive arms and hands. They instantly realized they couldn't help him, so they immediately turned and started to run. The giant male creature came out of the bushes and went charging into the two of them from behind. He knocked one of the men to the ground, and he was temporarily knocked unconscious. The other one began running for his life, but he was no match for the creature's speed. It hit him again from behind, but this time it knocked him several feet to the ground. Stunned, he knew he couldn't fight this ferocious creature, so he immediately got to his feet and started to run again. He hit the hiker from behind again, and this time he hit him with enough force that it shattered his right arm. He began screaming for his life and holding his arm. Seeing a cliff nearby, he got to his feet once again and headed for it. The creature seemed to be torturing him before it killed him as it charged at his legs and broke them in several places. He was only a few yards from the side of the cliff as the creature dragged his body to the edge. Before the next charge from the creature, the hiker rolled his body over the side. It was a forty-foot dropped straight down to the boulders below, but he knew he was spent and couldn't take another massive creature attack. Once it was over, the creature let out a thunderous bellowing cry, and the female answered him with her return cry.

While all of that was going on, the third climber that was temporarily knocked unconscious had gotten to his feet and started running. He ran down the trail and back toward the camp. The creatures were so preoccupied with their attack that they didn't notice he had escaped. He was terrified the creatures were going to come after him next as he kept running. He believed that any second, they were going to attack him from behind and crush him as they had done to the other two climbers. Everything had happened so fast, and he was hit from behind, so he didn't get a good look at the creature's face and thought they were just angry grizzly bears.

When he got back to the camp, he told everyone what had happened and that the bears may be coming their way. Everyone immediately packed up all their gear and headed back down out of the mountains. It was dark when they got to the bus, and everyone was freaked out as they loaded up and headed for town.

When they got into town, they went to the Sheriff's office and told Judy what had happened. They told her two grizzly bears had attacked three people in their group, and two of them may be dead. She could get Sheriff Kane on the phone, and he told her he would be there as soon as he could.

He got to his office about an hour later, and the hiker told him what had happened up by Sawtooth Ridge. The Sheriff told everyone he would form a search party in the morning, and they would go out and see what they could find. He made arrangements with a local hotel to take in the tourists while his search party looked for the hikers.

It was the early morning hours, and Sheriff Kane had contacted several men from town to check on the two missing hikers. Zak heard about the search, so he called the Sheriff and told him that he, Seth, and Julie would go out on the group's search party. Sheriff Kane welcomed the extra help.

Zak called Julie as soon as he heard about the missing hikers and the search party and said, "See, I told you those damn creatures are out there, now they've killed two hikers, but the Sheriff thinks it was a couple of grizzly bears. We have to get out there and stop them."

Julie replied, "Man, it's too bad we couldn't have done something to stop them from going out there in the first place, maybe given them some heads up."

Zak said, "It probably wouldn't have made a bit of difference, Julie. You know how those tourists are when they get here. They don't listen to anyone; they do their own thing. It's too late now for those poor guys, but maybe we can stop them from killing anyone else."

Zak and Julie told the Sheriff about the creatures, but they knew that talking to him about them during the search party wasn't the right time. Everyone in the search party was armed, and before they left, Sheriff Kane told everyone to be careful because they had two killer grizzlies on their hands, and it could get nasty if they run into them. Zak looked over at Julie and just rolled his eyes. They made it to the area where the hikers had been killed, and there were large amounts of blood in the trail, but nobodies. Zak figured the creatures had taken the two bodies back to the caves to feed on them as they had done with the Indian from the village. The search party continued the search for a few more days after the bus took the hikers back to Seattle but couldn't find any trace of the two men.

The monster killers had once again successfully searched for food because they had gotten a taste of human flesh and liked it. They were going to kill a lot more.

Chapter 11 - Timothy Wants to See the Creatures

Zak got a call from Timothy Melrose from the lab testing facility, and he told Zak he would be coming to the forest over the weekend so he could search for the two creatures and try to get up close to them. Zak couldn't believe what he was hearing from this guy. He thought, "He's either got his head buried in the sand, or he's just a total dumb ass. He can't get up close to them without being killed." Zak tried not to get upset with him as he asked, "So do you plan on just going out there in the forest all alone and with no weapons?"

Timothy replied, "Yes, my boss told me to go and check things out and try and get up close enough to the creatures to take a few photos of them. From all the reports we've ever heard about the indigenous Bigfoot over the years, they're not dangerous to humans and try to avoid any contact with them."

Zak chimed in and said, "Yes, that may have been true with the indigenous Bigfoots that everyone has seen in this area before, but haven't you heard about some of the missing people the creatures have killed around here? These creatures are different; they're killers."

Zak told him it wouldn't be a perfect time to go out in the woods alone right now because the creatures had recently mauled and killed a couple of tourists from Seattle, besides the Indian. "We still haven't found their bodies or any trace of them."

Zak was serious as he said, "If you go out there and get close enough to take pictures of them, they'll kill you."

Timothy laughed aloud and said, "Well, I guess I'll just have to take my chances."

Zak could see there was no talking to this dummy and told him that they would go out with him in the woods when he got to town to call him. He told Timothy, "Why don't you just stay at my house while you're here." Timothy quickly took him up on the offer. Zak was hoping that once Timothy got there, he could talk him out of the ridiculous notion of taking pictures of the creatures.

Immediately after they hung up the phone with each other, Zak called Seth and Julie and told them that they needed to go out with Timothy when he got there and try to keep him alive.

Seth asked, "Is he a nutcase; those creatures will kill him if we don't go with him."

Zak joked and said, "Yeah, maybe we should let him go out there, and the creatures could rip him from limb to limb." Then he laughed and said, "Just kidding, I wouldn't do that."

Timothy arrived at Zak's house around six on Friday night and was excited about going into the woods. Zak could tell he was a true city slicker. He had an expensive camera hanging around his neck and shoulder. He wasn't dressed to go out in the woods. He was wearing shorts, tennis shoes, and even though Zak had warned him, nothing to protect himself from the creatures. Zak thought he looked more like a bird watcher instead of a guy going out searching for a couple of deadly killers.

Later that night, after they had dinner and relaxed for a while, Timothy decided he wanted to take a stroll to the edge of the forest alone to see what it looked like in the woods. Zak sat on the sofa and said, "Go for it, but just remember, the creatures are out there somewhere, so keep an eye out for them." When he left the house, he enthusiastically jumped off the porch and almost skipped in the direction of the woods. He got about sixty yards away from the lights of the house when, for the first time, he felt just how creepy and scary it was in the pitch-black night alone. He could hardly see where he was going and suddenly felt as though he was being watched. He felt the hair on the back of his neck rise, and a chill came over his body. Standing there, frozen in fear, he now realized how vulnerable he was.

He looked around wide-eyed and said, "Oh, Shit," and quickly turned and ran as fast as he could go back to the house.

He was shaking and breathing heavy as Zak met him at the front door and said, "Everything Alright Timothy?"

Timothy squeaked out, "Yes, I'm fine."

The next day he had a lackadaisical attitude about the entire search when they got to the forest. He asked them if they were ready, and Seth just shook his head in disbelief as they headed into the woods. He was half-joking as he said, "How about we just send you out ahead of us as bait?" Everyone laughed, except Timothy.

The deeper they got into the forest, Timothy's demeanor changed. He was now becoming afraid of every sound they heard. He began to ask, "Hey guys, what was that, and hey guys, did you hear that. He was becoming spooked; even when the birds made a loud warning signal, he would yell out. At one point, they heard a loud cry from one of the creatures, and it was close. When they heard it, Timothy quickly retreated backward and let out a squeal. "What was that?" he asked.

"Just a little old killer creature," Seth replied.

Timothy said, "Oh, Shit. That was loud and creepy."

Julie walked over to him and put her arm around him, and said, "Take it easy, Timothy, we have our rifles with us, and if one of the creatures comes after you, we'll shoot it." His eyes were bugged out, and he had a frown on his face, and Julie could tell he was terrified.

They continued just a little further down the trail when they heard growls and snorts coming from the creatures as they chattered back and forth to each other. Timothy said, "To heck with this, guys, I think I'm done here. It's just too darn scary out here in the woods for me." Zak was a little relieved when Timothy said that because he didn't want to be responsible for Timothy if he was killed by one of the creatures. He knew that the creatures were so quick and agile; they could swoop him away before any of them could get an aim on them with their rifles.

The creatures followed them from a distance in the trees as the three made their way back. They could hear the breaking of tree limbs and twigs from the forest floor but couldn't see anything. The creatures stayed just far enough out of sight, not to be seen. Timothy kept saying, "How much further do we have to go to get out of these woods?"

Once they arrived back in town, they were standing around talking, and Timothy said, "Thank you, guys. I think that's one of the most frightening experiences I've ever been through in my life. I also think I'm going to take your advice, Zak. I'm going to stay out of the woods from now on. It's not my cup of tea." They all laughed, but it was more of a sigh of relief than what he had said.

Zak said, "You go back and tell your boss these creatures are real, and they're furious killers. We can't treat them like the other Bigfoot animals that have been here for hundreds of years. We have to hunt these down and kill them, or they'll end up killing a lot of people in the woods."

Timothy replied, "Yeah, I'll tell him to come down here and check them out for himself if he wants to, but I'm done with them."

After Timothy left, Zak and Julie ran into Sheriff Kane outside Bessie's restaurant, so Zak thought it would be the perfect opportunity to talk to him.

Zak asked him if they could talk to him for a minute, and he agreed as he said, "Come on in, let's talk inside."

Once the Sheriff had his coffee, he asked them what was on their minds. Zak asked, "Have you had any luck finding the two climbers?" He already knew what the Sheriff was going to say, but he wanted to get the Sheriff talking about their disappearance before telling him about Seth's near-fatal abduction. Zak asked, "Have you ever wondered what happened to Seth's dog, Rex?"

The Sheriff looked up from his coffee and stared Zak in the eyes as he said, "I just heard a large bear mauled him."

Zak shook his head back and forth, "Nope, that's not what happened. I was with Seth when Rex was killed."

He then began to tell Sheriff Kane all about the creatures and having the DNA tests done and everything. When he finished, Sheriff Kane chuckled and said, "That's one hell of a story Zak."

Zak angrily replied, "It's not a story, Sheriff, it's all true, and you can believe me and put together a search party to go after those two creatures and hunt them down and kill them, or you can keep pretending they are just a couple of big grizzly bears and get more people killed up in the woods." Sheriff Kane didn't believe in UFO's and Zak's account of what he and Seth had seen and experienced was just too much for him to accept.

As he got up from his chair, he threw a couple of bucks on the table for his coffee and said, "I'll have to think about everything you told me for a few days, Zak." He smirked on his way out and said under his breath, "UFO and Aliens, yeah, right."

After he left, Zak said to Julie, "Looks like we'll have to be the ones that hunt down those creatures because he sure in the hell isn't going to do anything about them. He has his head square up his butt."

Chapter 12 - He's Come Back!!

"Don, can you take out the trash pleassssse." Don stood up from his favorite easy chair and mumbled something under his breath. "You know, you mumble a lot when you speak to me," Gladys commented.

Don mumbled back, "No, I don't," as he walked toward the kitchen, not that they needed much verbal communication after 40 years of marriage. They were well synced.

Don headed out the side kitchen door with the trash bag in hand. As he stepped into the cool evening air, his senses immediately sprang alert. How he loved this part of the country, the distant rustle of the tall forest trees and the song of the different animals and insects mingled with the pleasant sound of the wind as it whistled through his property. The insects were unusually quiet around the house. Tonight, the wind carried a strong unpleasant pungent smell. Don couldn't place, almost like a dead decaying foul smell, which seemed to be strongest in the forest's direction next to his house. "Damn, must be a dead animal," Don thought as he sat the trash bag down and walked over to the south side of the house that faced the forest. As he got closer to the forest edge, he scanned as far as he could see and could see no fallen animal, but the foul smell permeated the area.

Further out into the dense forest, he could barely hear what he thought was some type of speech, like a chatter, but with a high-pitched snarl and low guttural belching sounds. Fearing that the creature he'd seen days before may be close, he slowly backed up while keeping his eyes on the tree line. And then it stepped out from being well hidden behind an enormous Redwood tree. The creature stepped side-ways and into full view of Don.

The early evening light was still present and shone directly onto the hulking figure, and Don was able to see the creature's complete detail for the first time. The size was the dominating feature. Standing over 8 feet tall and possibly weighing over 800 pounds, it was massive. Its body was covered by longish hair spread from top to feet bottom. The hands, interestingly enough, though large, were very human-like but sported fingernails or claws that looked to be at least 6 inches long. The genitalia was not visible because of the hair length. On each side of the head was a small ear covered with hair or fur. The most compelling feature was the creature's face, which was exceptionally large and nearly devoid of hair, was characteristically human-looking, only more menacing and full of fury.

The creature's mouth, which had been closed, pursed to a slight growl, and then it opened its mouth in total, and Don could see the teeth protrude much like the creature had a snout and projected the teeth slightly forward. The incisors were very pronounced and fang-like, while the rest of the teeth looked humanoid, but once again, large.

As the creature stood there, it slowly closed and then opened its mouth again and then again, leaving it open as it gazed at Don. Upon initially seeing the creature, Don froze, and for a full minute, the two stared at each other. Then Don mumbled, "He's come back," and at that moment, the creature yelled an incredible roar that Don could feel vibrate in his chest 20 feet away.

Don immediately turned and ran back to his house. Being without any weapons, he was scared shitless.

At that exact moment, he heard his wife Gladys hysterically yell, "He's back," and upon hearing her, he felt strangely startled, almost as much as being confronted by the creature. In over 40 years of marriage, he had never heard his wife scream so hysterically.

Don met Gladys at the side door and forced her in so quickly she fell inside partially on her back as Don scrambled to the living room to grab his rifle. As Gladys was rising to lock the door, it shattered into several pieces and flew inward, once again throwing her backward and leaving her disoriented and badly shaken. As she started to rise again, her eyes moved upward, and standing in her doorway, breathing heavy and frenzied, was a huge female creature.

As the female creature stepped into the house, the male followed and pushed past Gladys toward Don in the living room. Seeing the weapon in Dons hands, it raked its massive arm against the kitchen table, which flew into the living room wall shattering into several pieces, missing Don by mere feet and causing him and the 308 rifle to scatter in opposite directions. "Fuck you," Don yelled as he worked his way to his feet, grabbing one of the still intact legs of the shattered kitchen table for a weapon as the creature moved toward him.

Don yelled out, "Gladys get to the attic," As he raised his wooden weapon for the advance of the male creature. In a state of absolute shock, Gladys sprang to her feet, screaming horribly at the top of her lungs. The female creature, which had been facing the living room watching the carnage develop, merely turned and looked at Gladys, who was running and stumbling to the house's stairwell, with an amused look on its face.

Gladys got to the top of the stairs and stood a moment shaking uncontrollably and trying to grab a breath. Far below, she could hear her husband screaming and cursing along with thrashing and banging sounds of things being thrown against walls. Quickly, Gladys ran up the last stairs to the attic doorway, threw it open, and closing it behind her without remembering to lock it.

The sounds in the downstairs rooms were now long silent, except for the faint sound of a radio in her master bedroom, softly blaring out the rhythms of a popular pop song and the now louder thump, thump, of Footfalls on the Stairs. The handle of the attic door was one that Gladys had bought at Pier 1 imports in Seattle and was a faux antique. It slowly turned, and Gladys once again was met with the face of the female monster, a face that was now full of fury and bloodlust.

Chapter 13 - Seth Disappears

The following weekend Seth and Zak talked on the phone, and Zak told him he had to check on his sister and her family. He told Seth he would tell Vera and William about the creatures to protect themselves if they were to be confronted by them.

He told Seth his sister wanted him to spend the night to be gone a couple of days. He asked Julie if she wanted to go with him, and to his surprise, she said she wanted to go along. She loved Vera and Kari and looked forward to the visit. Zak was looking forward to spending some good quality relaxing time with Julie instead of hunting for the creatures.

Zak said, "Look, Seth, I know you, and you aren't going to want to keep from hunting those creatures, but don't go out into the woods by yourself. Those things will kill you."

Seth made a promise he wasn't sure he could keep as he crossed his fingers and replied, "I won't. I'll wait for you guys to get back. Have a good time together. You guys need it."

When the weekend came around, Seth was sitting home by himself, and he began to think about losing Rex and started getting angry that the creature had killed him. He had been Seth's best friend and only companion ever since he got him as a puppy. While he was sitting around thinking about what happened to Rex, he had a few tears in his eyes as he whispered, "Hey boy, thanks for protecting me from those creatures and saving my life." He clenched his right fist and hit the wall, "I'm not going to sit here all weekend and not go out looking for those bastards. I want them dead." He wasn't thinking about his safety or being killed by the creatures; he just felt that he wanted to get revenge for what they had done to his best friend.

It was still early in the morning, and rationale had left him as he dressed in his camouflage clothing for going into the woods and grabbed his rifle and pistol. He wasn't going to let anyone know that he was going out into the woods alone; he was thinking only about his mission of revenge.

When he arrived at the woods, it had been taped off at the trails' entry, and danger signs were posted to keep hikers and rock climbers out. They said, "Danger, Killer bears in the woods. Stay out." Seth thought, "Well, at least Sheriff Kane is doing something to try and keep people out of the woods. Maybe that'll help a little."

As he made his way onto Mildred Trail, he moved quickly in the lower flats where there were no bush and trees. He had been on this trail hundreds of times since he was a kid and knew it well. As he got closer to where the creatures had killed Rex, he put his rifle in both hands and began looking carefully in all directions as he slowly moved along. He occasionally would turn around and look over his shoulders just in case the creatures were trying to sneak up behind him. It was quiet, and he felt like it was eerie and spooky being out there alone. He felt as though he could hear his heartbeat because it was beating heavy and fast the deeper he got into the woods. His hands had become a little sweaty from gripping the rifle a little tight, and so he had to wipe the sweat on his pants.

Then he spotted the creatures, and they were on the trail a reasonable distance from him. They were walking briskly along, and it looked like they were in a hurry to get back to their hiding place. They had their heads lowered, looking toward the ground, and had not heard or seen him yet. The female had her long arms swinging out in front of her and then back behind her. The male creature had a good size Black-tailed deer over his shoulder, and they were making their way up toward the caves. Seth thought, "At least it's not another human they're going to eat this time. As soon as I can get a little closer, and they are in an open clearing, I will shoot those monsters, and then we'll be done with them." He foolishly believed he could kill them both before one of them had a chance to retaliate against his first shot at them. When he saw them, all reasoning had left him, and the anger took over.

He increased his pace and got up a little closer to the creatures, and now he was only about two hundred yards behind them. Suddenly, the male creature stopped in his tracks, looked back down the trail, and smelled in the air. By then, Seth had ducked behind the cover of the trees. He whispered, "Ok, now I may not have any choice. I may have to start shooting them, especially if they come after me." He felt like he was not quite close enough to get a good shot off at both, so he waited to see where they were headed and if he could get a better shot at them. After a minute, he peeked out from around the trees, and the creatures decided to continue up the trail. He kept waiting for just the right opportunity to take his shots as fear set in, and he thought, "Maybe I will only be able to kill one of them, and the other one will come after me, and I wouldn't be able to kill it." Then the fear left him for a second, and he shifted back to his mission, "I have to kill these things before they make it up there to the caves. Once they get in there, then I'll lose my opportunity."

They moved so fast that Seth decided to take a shot at the male creature while he was still out in the open. The bullet just missed him as it zinged by his head, and he turned back toward Seth and let out a deep, bellowing scream. He then quickly turned around and met up with the female that had continued walking. Seth was trying to get an aim on him again when the creatures suddenly ducked into a hole in the ground to a hidden cave entrance that Seth didn't know was there.

They weren't using the caves on the mountains' side to live in, like he, Zak, and others thought they were using this underground cave system instead. They had merely taken Benjamin's brother's body to the upper cave and ate him to throw the humans off their trail. Seth thought, "Man, these creatures must be pretty smart to fool everyone, including the search parties that were looking for them." Their actual hiding place was deep in the ground. Everyone had been hunting for them in the caves on the side of the mountains. Zak and Seth had lived in the area all their lives and didn't know this underground cave entrance was there until the creatures disappeared into it.

Seth lost his opportunity to kill the creatures, but at least he got a shot at the male and now knew where they had been hiding. He was disappointed in himself for not hitting the creature with his bullet, as he turned and began to head out of the woods before it got dark. He whispered, "Sorry, Rex, I'll get them next time, boy."

When he got back down to the bottom of Sawtooth Ridge, something strange happened. It was eerily like his first encounter with the UFO when another UFO came zooming out of the sky and stopped abruptly about twenty feet directly above him. As it sat there hovering, it made some type of humming noise, and the bottom of the craft opened. A bright beam of light shot down over Seth, and he was instantly paralyzed in place. He felt himself being lifted into the light and inside the craft. He tried to fight it but was powerless to stop what was happening to him. He could open his mouth, so he tried to scream, but his voice was silent. He was no longer in control of any part of his body.

Once inside the craft, the bottom floor closed, and three alien beings met him and took him down a hallway to a room that resembled an operating room. They immediately laid him on a bright gleaming metal table and strapped him down. He felt as though he was in some dream-like state as he looked up at the creatures, and he thought, "These guys look just like all the pictures and movies I've seen of aliens since I was a kid."

They had a large head, no mouth or nose, and nostrils, just a tiny bump. No ears and no hair. Their hands had five thin fingers but appeared to be completely smooth, as was the rest of their body, which had a grayish tint. Their eyes were large and black, like large black marbles. And then it hit him; the aliens were wearing a bodysuit or mask. They were communicating with him through some form of mental telepathy, and their eyes were not moving. (The aliens had mastered telepathy in its truest form and used it to communicate with humans when the humans are abducted). He wondered what they looked like under the suit they were wearing. As he struggled to free himself, one of them told him to relax; they weren't going to hurt him.

Once he was secured on board, the craft shot up instantly and had entered the vastness of space. Two of the aliens moved closer to Seth, and he could now see the fullness and design of the spacesuit worn by the aliens. No longer needing to wear the suit inside their craft, the third alien standing in the back began to remove his suit. Interestingly enough, it seemed to Seth that the aliens were smaller in size and stature than when they had been when they first abducted him, not knowing that once they entered into space, the alien's bodies (because of the difference in gravity) morphed into a smaller being. The suit material was sleek and very flexible and reminded Seth of the material he had read about what they found at the alleged Roswell crash site. Almost alloy, yet soft fabric.

From all accounts, nothing could prepare Seth for the suits removed disclosure. We, humans, see a spacesuit as those worn by astronauts on the Apollo and Russian crewed missions, and we approach our view from that perspective. These suits were as a second skin and, once removed, revealed the true image of the alien underneath. They had the likeness of Humans (or we in the likeness of them). Though smaller, they had a mouth, normal eyes, slightly larger and more oval — a nose with nostrils and ears with canals and a semblance of a silky type of hair. The heads were more bulbous and larger than humans, but the features were remarkably similar.

The spacesuit, which covered their body, merely made it appear smooth and hairless and without facial features giving them the appearance of the commonly known "grey" alien. Their body was a pale white color with spindly legs, arms, and torso (possibly due to their planet's low or no gravitational pull). The suit also covered and made smooth their hands and fingers, which now showed definition and ligature.

Much to Seth's surprise, even in his tranquilized state the aliens had put him in, he saw that they were human-like, just like him. Seeing the similarity to humans somewhat helped him relax as two of the aliens began to do extractions of blood and sperm as they stuck long needles into his groin area, but he never felt the pain of it.

Seth asked them why they were doing that to him and why they had dropped off the two deadly creatures in the woods at Skokomish Forest. He told them the creatures had been killing and abducting people in the forest.

The alien said, "They are experimental beings, and we're hoping they are more immune to the viruses and bacteria on Earth. Throughout the years, we have brought back some of the viruses and bacteria to our planet. They have killed a lot of our people. These beings are test subjects because we need to determine if they are resistant to viruses and bacteria. We need to let them live down there for several months before we can take them back and test them to see if they are free of the diseases."

Seth said, "Hey, to hell with that, those creatures are killers, and they'll be dead before you guys pick them up. We'll kill every last one of them you unleash down here on us." The aliens stepped back when he said that, as if they were surprised, he would take that type of defensive posture toward their test subjects.

He told Seth, "The humans are destroying their planet. If they don't do something to stop the destruction, they will destroy it with nuclear bombs or something else, affecting the entire universe. We cannot let that happen; we've been trying to save you from creating your demise. You don't have any respect for your beautiful planet and what it does for you."

Right after the alien said that, Seth passed out, and the next thing he remembered was waking up at the entrance to the forest. He had been gone for four days, but he thought it was just a few minutes. His rifle and pistol were lying next to him on the ground, but he had no recollection of the extraction of blood and sperm. However, he did have a few slightly painful small holes where they had inserted the needles into his body.

Once he got home. He found out that Julie and Zak had spent the last few days looking for him and figuring out what happened to him. They believed he went into the woods alone, and the creatures had taken him and killed him. They even reported him as missing to Sheriff Kane.

Although he had a lot of memory loss for what had happened to him, he did remember what the aliens told him about the creatures and the destruction of Earth by humans. He would rest up a few days and then tell Julie and Zak what he could remember about his unbelievable journey into space with the aliens and what they told him.

Chapter 14 - Talking to Dr. Johnathon Weir

It was about two weeks after Timothy's visit to the Skokomish Wilderness when Zak got a call from him and told him the testing facility's results had come back. He was extremely excited as he began talking about what they had found in the tests. He had Zak's attention when he said, "We did two types of tests on the samples, a modern human mtDNA and novel nuDNA, and the results indicate that the creature is a hybrid species. The result of a male grizzly bear, some homo sapiens, and also a third DNA sequence that we can't identify."

"We've never seen anything like this before, so it would've had to have been genetically altered by someone or something. The connection to the grizzly bear is probably why they are so aggressive toward humans. Now, didn't you say that these creatures came out of a UFO or a flying craft?"

"Yes," Zak replied.

"Well, that 3rd DNA sequence could be alien, and that could also mean they're probably highly intelligent."

Zak said aloud, "I knew it. I figured they are part alien, and they're the ones that, for some reason, genetically altered and made those creatures." He thanked Timothy for the information and couldn't wait to get off the phone and find Seth and tell him the tests' results.

Before hanging up, Timothy told Zak about a professor by the name of Dr. Johnathon Weir, and he wanted him to talk to him on the phone. Timothy said he was a renowned astronomer, professor, cryptozoologist and ufologist, that has been doing extensive research on the UFO phenomenon for years and would be a great person to talk to regarding their UFO story.

Zak got his number from Timothy and, later that day, called several times before he was able to make an appointment to talk to him on the phone. Once they made the connection, they spoke for nearly an hour. During their conversation, Zak told him about Seth's recent abduction, and he told Zak he was not surprised because abduction reports were happening all over Earth.

He told Zak he had done extensive research regarding the UFOs that had been spotted throughout the National forests over the years and had been trying to see if he could find out more about them. During his research, he found there were accounts and theories of all kinds regarding the extraterrestrials in that area.

He told Zak, "There are seven species of aliens that have been coming to earth from habitable planets scattered throughout the universe, some even in parallel universes. They are highly intelligent beings with much higher intelligence than humans."

Zak thought, "They wouldn't have to be too smart to be more intelligent than a lot of people I know."

"Their language is a geometric rhythm that is so highly advanced that humans can't figure out. They use it to communicate with each other and species from other planets."

Zak also thought, "Man, this guy is way out there, but it does make sense. We have our different languages here on earth. How did we get all those?"

He told Zak about the Nazca Lines in Peru, where the aliens tried to communicate with humans thousands of years ago with their lines in the ground. Recently they have been attempting to communicate with us by showing their signs in fields. He said, "We are so far behind them that we haven't been able to figure out the messages; we just call them "crop circles."

The more he told Zak about aliens and UFOs, the deeper he got into some of the more detailed information. One of the things that intrigued Zak the most was that he said, "They are advanced in physics and have learned how to manipulate air travel with their flying craft. They use time warp drive and wormholes and travel through space anywhere they want to go in a short period. They can go to places it would take our present-day primitive craft thousands of years to get to in just a matter of days or months. They can accelerate with g. Forces too strong for the human body to withstand. They can also reach hypersonic speed with no heat trails or sonic booms, and their craft seems to resist the effects of the earth's gravity." That made a lot of sense to Zak, so when Seth said he saw the alien craft zoom right up to the bottom of the mountain, hover there, let the creatures off, and took off in warp speed, he now came in crystal clear to Zak.

Zak always wondered about the pyramids and what their purpose could have been, so he asked Professor Weir his opinion about them.

He said, "In the distant past, the aliens built all the pyramids in different earth locations and along certain parallels. They used their mental abilities to maneuver the huge stones into place, and the pyramids were used as energy beacons for their flying machines. They could reenergize their craft on earth without having to return to their planet to get more energy. Once they found a way to harness the sun's energy rays, they no longer needed the pyramids' energy source and abandoned them. Now the pyramids are just ancient monuments to a distant past long gone."

"Some of the different alien species first started coming to earth to mine for the precious gold that was abundant on earth. In such demand by the aliens, the different species fought over it in the distant past. They had wars in space. They almost destroyed each other with their nuclear, laser, and other advanced weapons before they made a peace agreement not to annihilate each other.

One species of the aliens brought their workers down to earth, which we now call Bigfoot, to help harvest the heavy gold. That is why so many sightings of the creatures have been seen all over the earth. Not known to human knowledge yet, but when one of the creatures is injured or shot, there is a signal transmitted to their nearest craft, and it instantly comes and picks them up. That is why none of the creatures or their bones have ever been found on earth.

About 4,600 years ago, the aliens saw how primitive the people of earth were, and so to improve the intelligence and adaptability of humans, they genetically manipulated the genes of humans and introduced a new chromosome to the human DNA. Since that time, we have had the sudden emergence of "Modern Man." They are conducting several types of tests on their test subjects. They started abducting humans and doing artificial crossbreeding between their species and humans to produce a perfect hybrid. Most of the abductees have reported having invasive medical procedures performed on their reproductive systems. According to what they told your cousin Seth while he was aboard their craft, they found that their species was not immune to the viruses and bacteria on earth, and they didn't have any natural adaption against them. It sounds like they are trying to rectify that problem by creating their hybrid species of human, grizzly, and alien that will be immune to the diseases. If they are resistant, they will have a natural adaptation that humans have to the planet earth.

Also, their biological code gives them extremely potent psychic abilities. They have a natural ability with the world but bonded to the aliens. With the result of their new experiment, the offspring are being bred to serve, possibly as an individual with no compassion, respect, or empathy for humanity. They look at humans as mere inferior animals. Although the creatures are not always hostile and harmful to human children, the new species may be devastating killers to the adults of our species."

Zak thanked Professor Weir for all his information and perspective on everything and said, "If you want to talk to me again about your aliens, then just give me a call, and we can discuss it further." Zak told him if something new came up, he would.

Once they hung up, Zak said, "Man, that was an interesting conversation. I never expected to hear all that." He thought, "It sounds like during one of their experimentations that they crossed a grizzly bear to bigfoot and the DNA from their species. Not knowing how the being would react on earth, they decided to create a male and female and drop them into the remote forest of the Skokomish wilderness. They unleashed the killers right in our backyard."

Zak leaned back on his couch and rubbed his face with his hands, resting his head on the top of the cushion. He stared up to the ceiling, exhaling his breath as he softly said aloud, "Man, I need your help on this one, Grandpa," And slowly closed his eyes and fell to sleep.

Chapter 15 - Days Long Gone

"911. What is your emergency?" (pause) "911. What is your emergency?" (Highly excited)

"Yeah, I wanna report an intruder walking around my backyard!"

"You have a person walking through your yard?"

(Frustrated), "Yeah, someone is walking all around my yard, and he's big, and my dogs are going crazy. GET SOMEONE OUT HERE NOW?

"Is it a male or a female?" "I don't know it's a man, DAMMIT, he's looking at me right now."

"Is he in your yard?"

"Yes, and he is big. The son of a bitch is big. Get someone out here now!"

Zak had asked Sheriff Kane to meet him at Bessie's Diner, which sat on Main Street's corner in Lilliwaup. Seth had been missing for four days, and Zak was not only confounded but upset and just figured that Seth had gone into the forest seeking revenge for Rex's death. He felt he needed to reach out to the sheriff and tell him again what he knew and convince him there were creatures in those woods. "I think Seth went in there and was taken by them, so I need you to set up a search party to look for him."

"Zak, look, I hear you. I think Seth's missing too, and yes, he may have gone into those woods, but taken my monsters?"

"Creatures. Ok, creatures, monsters, whatever. Zak, we have a bear problem. There's a couple of big bears that have partnered up, and they are on a rampage.

That's it? Killer bears?

I'll get the bastards. I know where you're going with this, and believe me at one time, I too loved an adventure."

It might have been different in another life, and in another life, I might have done something similar, but those days are gone, long, long, gone. These days it's in the book, and we have a bear problem."

Zak, who was staring straight ahead as the sheriff spoke, turned his head to face Kane. "You gotta problem alright, Phillip, and it's not Bears. To hell with it, I'll take care of it myself."

As he stood up and made for the door, the sheriff yelled behind him, "Don't do anything stupid, Zak, by the book. BY THE BOOK." Sheriff Kane reached for his phone, which squawked,"

Sheriff, we have a 911 call. The bear is back."

Kane rose from his chair, "I'm on my way."

Chapter 16 - Camping

One of the major misconceptions that people who live in large cities have when they enter the forest is, they believe it is an extension of their comfortable enabled life. That is why some embrace the opportunity to go camping.

They feel it gives them the chance to step outside of their tightly wound structure and loosen up and relax before returning once again refreshed to their structured lives. But there lies the rub; it is not an extension; it is foreign soil. It is the wild and the place of alternate lifestyles. It is the home of wild animals, and when we step into the wild, we step into their yard.

Marcus, at 35 years old, was at his peak in his strengths. He had a strong physical presence, a strong sense of direction, a strong commitment to the love of his life, his girlfriend, Mary. He had a strong and focused desire to become the first person to photograph indeed or film a real Bigfoot and prove their existence.

He and Mary were loaded into his Ford Escape with all his gear and all that implied. But how he had talked Mary into going on this adventure with him, he'll never know. Well, she loved him, right?

Their destination is the Olympic National Park in Washington state. Ground 0 for the highest number of sightings of the Bigfoot encounters in America. He had googled several areas on the internet where many people had sighted the big guy in the Olympic National Park and narrowed one choice down to a place called the Skokomish region.

Living in Palo Alto, California, he'd planned this more as a road trip than as a one-stop destination. They had stopped in Willow Creek in Northern California and had the famous Bigfoot burger in the restaurant next to their hotel and stayed on the Gold Coast of Oregon to favor Mary. They were sleeping at an overly priced but charming bed and breakfast, situated right on a cliff's edge, overlooking the beautiful Pacific Ocean.

But his end goal was to camp in the thick forest of the Olympic Park, nestled in a cozy spot in their tent, listening to the soothing night sounds of nature and a serene comfort in knowing he was at one with nature.

Pulling into the park's entrance and driving in several miles, he was instantly struck with the realization of how dense and foliaged these forests are. Not unlike the forest of Northern California that he'd grown up hiking and traversing, but these were so green and highly populated with huge ferns and immense trees whose base had exposed roots as thick as a full-grown tree, it was beautiful.

"If Bigfoot can live anywhere, it is here," he thought. He was almost giddy. He drove for miles and miles, and the scenery never changed. And how dense, only being able to see within the forest a few feet from the road.

As an opening finally cleared, they could see signs showing a town ahead called Lilliwaup and decided to stop there before heading into the high wilderness area of Skokomish. The town was small but pronounced, obviously having been populated for many years. Their first stop was for food, and the little diner on the corner looked like it would just fill the bill.

"Bessie's Diner," Marcus said as they stepped through the aged front door. The ring of the entry bell chimed at that moment in perfect unison with the ching of the cash register as a patron turned to depart, having paid his bill. "Perfect," said Marcus. "I feel the vibe, and these people are Bigfootist; they are here where it's all happening." As they made their way to an empty table.

Mary only laughed and said, "Not another Bigfoot burger, please."

They reached their destination by early evening and decided to park the car at the farthest possible point before having to hike in another several mile to a stream shown on their GPS. Their gear was easily carried, and they arrived at their end spot before it began to grow dark.

"I'm going to set up the tent right away. Let's not burn a fire tonight, and that way, we can head out early in the morning and hike a little further in."

"Sounds good. I'm beat. First, throw me the Skittles," Mary replied.

That night was nowhere how Marcus imagined it would go. The sounds of the night were electric, and everything was amplified. A screech of an owl became a cry of a Banshee. They heard a loud knock in the distance, and Marcus swore it was off a tree.

After staying up the entire night and finally closing their eyes in the early morning hours, Mary startled awake and yelled, "Marcus. Marcus." But Marcus was gone.

Chapter 17 - The Battle

The cave system that travels under the Pacific Northwest is extensive, but unless you are a spelunker or geologist, it is relatively unknown to the general population. Most people who enter these caves are curious tourists who either happen upon them or have been told about them by others, and they rarely venture very far for fear of getting lost or the unknown, and that is for a good reason.

These caves not only can twist and turn for miles but are the living quarters of large and wild animals. One being the cougar or commonly called mountain lion. This large cat can grow to over 150 pounds and has been known to kill and eat humans. Also smaller, but just as ferocious, are the lynx that, when cornered, becomes a formidable foe.

The king of the hill would be the Grizzly Bear. This massive animal is vicious and fearsome when cornered or crossed, not meeting in a dark, cramped cave passage. These animals are truly monsters. Growing upward of 12 feet and weighing in over 1500 pounds, they maim humans and eat them while still alive. But the ones that had been seen in the Skokomish wilderness area were typically smaller, standing at on average between seven to eight feet and 600 to 700 pounds.

The creatures knew that their brethren creature was similar but also quite different. Very feral and less calculated. At times, a cumbersome being, but extremely deadly. And the creatures took measures to avoid and not confront them, but that was not always the case.

The hierarchy was in the creature's favor, and they were more intelligent and far crueler, and more homicidal. Such was when the creatures arrived back at the cave entrance, the large male carrying the lifeless bloodied body of Marcus on its shoulder.

Stepping into the entrance of the cave, the male heard the low, ominous growl of the enormous grizzly, drawn in by the fresh smell of the creatures' previous bloodied kill. The male, feeling his already heightened fury rise to rage, dropped the body to the ground and readied himself for the ensuing battle. The grizzly loomed forward and, seeing the entrance blocked by the creatures and the height and presence of the huge male, rose himself up to his full height of 7 feet, his head nearly touching the top of the cave, and took a running lunge at the male.

The female creature moved forward to stand side by side with the male, but the male raised his right arm to assuage her decision and immediately took a step forward, taking the lead in advance. The two giants met with a force that shook the cave space. The grizzly was bellowing the entire time.

The force momentarily stunned the grizzly, but just enough for the creature to grab the grizzly by the arm and slam it with a massive blow against the cave wall. Surprisingly the grizzly came back up with froth and blood flowing from its mouth and slung its large clawed paw at the male, which raked its shoulder and left a superficial imprint. It enraged the female who lunged at the grizzly and bit it viciously at the side of its neck. The male taking advantage of this brief respite, met eye contact with the grizzly's eyes, and with a furious blow, hit the bear in the head with such force it nearly severed the grizzly's head.

The two creatures stood over the torn and battered body of the grizzly, then lifting their faces to look at each other, and both smiled, their fangs shining bloody and victorious.

Chapter 18 - The Last Hunt with Ben

Zak, Seth, and Julie decided they would go back to the Indian village and see if Ben wanted to go with them to the underground cave where Seth had last seen the creatures duck into when he went out alone looking for them. They left early in the morning, the air was crisp, and they were equipped with several flashlights and, of course, their weapons. In a backpack, they carried a sack lunch for each of them and one for Ben.

On the way to the village, Zak said, "Have you noticed how strange it is out here? There isn't much wildlife in the woods like we usually see and hear. The creatures have scared everything away from here. They must have moved to another part of the forest. Even the birds in the trees sound different, and it's like they're afraid of something too because they're squawking and flying from tree to tree as if they're scared of something."

Seth angrily replied, "Those damn creatures are going to ruin our forest if we don't get rid of them soon."

When they first got to the village, it was quiet, and not very many people were scurrying around. Zak wondered if the creatures had been back and taken more of Ben's people. Seth found Ben and told him about their plan, and asked if he wanted to go along.

Zak was looking around and said, "Hey Ben, where is everybody? What's going on?"

Ben replied, "It's a quiet time in the Reservation. We have it from time to time, and everyone stays inside and does a lot of praying and aligning themselves with God. We do a lot of meditation and don't come out much until it's over. It usually lasts a week or two."

Julie said, "I like that. Too bad, we don't do it."

Ben strapped on his rifle, grabbed his walking stick, and said he was ready when he said, "Let's go get those monsters."

They connected with Mildred Trail and headed for their destination. They were deep in the woods when they heard a faint scream from a woman out in the distance. Zak had everyone stop while they listened to see if they could hear her again. A few minutes later, they heard the woman screaming once again. The group cautiously headed in the direction of the screams, and as they got closer, they saw the young woman, and she was frantically running through the woods and searching for her boyfriend.

When she saw them, she went running up to them and screamed out, "Have you seen my boyfriend, Marcus?" Julie could calm her down long enough to find out her name was Mary and tell her what happened. She told them they had been camped out not too far from there because her boyfriend wanted to get a picture of Bigfoot. When she woke that morning, he was gone, and she had been searching for him ever since.

Zak spoke up and said, "There are a couple of creatures that are loose in the forest that have been killing people. They're monsters, and they like the taste of humans, so I hope they haven't gotten your boyfriend."

At first, she didn't believe him, and she thought he was trying to scare her.

Then Julie said, "No, it's true, they are out there somewhere, and we're searching for them so we can kill them." Mary looked at the rifles and pistols they were carrying and then began to believe what Julie said.

She immediately yelled out, "Oh My God," sat down on the ground, and began to cry. She was sobbing as she said, "I hope they haven't killed him."

Zak replied, "You're just lucky they didn't get you too, running around out here alone in the forest. They must not be hungry right now."

Julie said, "We're heading a little further up the trail to a spot that goes down into a cave. We believe the creatures are hiding in there, so we're going after them. We're going to try and kill them. We don't have time to take you back right now, so you have to go along with us. I'm sorry, but we're not giving up on this hunt. We've come too far to turn back now." She also felt they were lucky to have Ben with them and knew if they turned back in the middle of their hunt, they might not be able to get him to go with them the next time.

As she sat on the ground, Mary looked up in the sky and yelled, "Am I in a bad dream or something? None of this can be real, can it?"

Seth helped her to her feet and said, "I'm afraid so, come on, we have to get moving." Seth asked her if she knew how to use a gun, and she said no.

Ben took the lead as the group headed toward the opening of the cave. When they got there, Zak said, "Man, I've been coming up here all my life, and I didn't know this entrance was here."

Seth replied, "Yeah, me either. It surprised me, too, when I saw the creatures slip in here."

Ben said, "I'll go in first, and then each of you follow me. If I see something that looks like the creatures, I'll take a shot. Each one of them carefully climbed several feet to the bottom of the cave, and Mary was clinging to the back of Seth's shirt as she stepped gingerly along. She was shaking with fear, too scared to say anything." Even though the rest had guns, they were hoping that would be enough to stop the massive creatures.

They were all a little uneasy as they turned on their flashlights and slowly made their way deeper into the cave system. Ben said, "Looks like it goes on for miles."

Julie said, "Man, it stinks down here; it smells like a dead animal or something."

Seth said, "Yeah, dead animal is right, a human animal."

They weren't giving up their hunt as they continued deeper into the cave. They had gone about a half-mile in when Ben had everyone stop. He had his flashlight pointed at a rounded-out area in the cave, and he could see parts of clothing lying on the ground. He whispered to Zak, "Get ready. I think those creatures are nearby because I see what's left of a couple of bodies over there." He flashed his light in the direction for them to see. "Keep the girls back until I check it out."

As he carefully approached and bent over the bodies, he could tell two bodies had been stripped clean of flesh and one recent body that just had parts of the flesh missing. "Ben said, "This is it. It is where they're bringing their kill. Be careful because they're probably somewhere nearby." Zak and Seth started to shine their flashlights all around. They had stayed back about thirty feet with the girls. That's when the male creature let out a ferocious cry, and it echoed throughout the cave. It was so close the girls both instinctively screamed out in fear.

Just as Ben looked up, the male creature hit him with a killing blow to the head. Ben went down, and the creature scooped him up with one arm and began to whisk him away. Because it was so dark in the cave, Zak and Seth couldn't get a good aim at the creature, but they fired several shots in its direction. The female creature then let out a bellowing scream, and it sounded like she was a little further into the cave system.

They each took a couple more shots in her direction before turning to the girls, and Zak said, "Let's get the hell out of here." Something the girls were more than happy to do. As they retreated, Zak and Seth walked backward with their rifles pointed back in the direction of the creatures and dark parts of the cave. They were able to make it out without another attack, but they had lost their friend, Ben. They were angry and disappointed as they walked back to Ben's village and told Walker what had happened to him.

While on the way there, Zak asked Mary what color of clothes Marcus had been wearing the night before, and she told him. Zak said he thought he recognized some of his clothing colors lying on the ground next to a half-eaten body in the cave. He told her Marcus was probably the latest person the creatures killed and took back to the caves.

Mary screamed out in pain, "Marcus."

On the way out of the forest, Zak said, "I'm not going to let these creatures beat us. They may have won this time, but we'll get them out in the open next time, and then we'll kill them." He wondered if Sheriff Kane would believe them now.

Chapter 19 - Don and Gladys sons try for Revenge

Don and Glady Daniels's two sons had been trying to get in touch with their parents for a few days without any luck. Randy was from Portland, Oregon, and he talked to one of his parents on the cell phone almost every day. And he'd been trying for three days to get in touch with them and wasn't able to get an answer. He talked to his brother Karl, who lived in Boise, Idaho, a couple of times and told him about his concerns. Karl, too, had been trying to contact his parents without any luck. Karl suggested, "Why don't we call the Sheriff department in the town of Lilliwaup and see if he could go out and check on them for us?"

Randy thought that was a good idea, so after he got off the phone with Karl, he called Sheriff Kane's office and talked to Judy. He told her that he hadn't heard from his parents in a few days, which was very unusual for them because they spoke to each other almost every day. He told her he was having a funny feeling something was wrong, so he asked her if she could have the Sheriff go out and check on them and see if they were ok. He left his phone number and asked if the Sheriff could call him back once he had checked things out.

When Sheriff Kane got to the office, he saw the note that he needed to check on Don and Gladys Daniels. He impatiently whispered, "Not them again; I wonder what's going on now?" He threw the note on his desk and forgot about it for the rest of the morning. It was right after lunch when Judy asked him if he got a chance to check on Don and Gladys.

He knew it was something he had to respond to and couldn't just push aside. Besides, he was caught up on his paperwork, so it would be an excellent time to drive by and see what was going on with them.

When he first got to their property, he noticed the animals were yelling for food and water, and it looked like they had been left alone a few days. As he drove down the driveway, he notices something strange. The front door was wide open, but he couldn't tell why or for how long. As he got closer, he thought, "Something is going on here, both cars are here, and their front door looks like it's been busted in from the outside."

He slowly got out of his car, pulled his pistol, and started calling out to Don and Gladys and wasn't getting any response. He walked around on the outside of the house and saw that the animals hadn't been fed for a few days. They were begging him for food and water.

Not seeing anything unusual on the outside, he made his way to the front door, and as soon as he looked inside, he said, "What the hell, something crushed that door like it was nothing." He saw the blood on the walls and the furniture that was crushed. He spotted the parcel body of Don lying on the living room floor. His flesh had been ripped from his body like it had been partially eaten. He immediately called Judy to send in reinforcements, and he kept searching the house when he saw bloodstains coming from the attic, and right below was the mutilated body of Gladys that had been dragged out of the attic and half-eaten. He whispered, "That isn't something a normal Grizzly would do. There is something else going on here. A grizzly would've dragged them off and eaten them in the woods." He was starting to wonder if some of Zak's story may be true.

He waited for backup as he went back outside and stood there by his patrol car, scratching his head. Once they took pictures and inspected the scene, he called the coroner's office to come and get what was left of the two bodies.

When he got back to the office, he took a few minutes to collect himself and then called Randy and gave him the bad news about the "Grizzly's" that had killed his parents. He told Randy that someone from his office would go by and feed and water the animals until he and his brother could get there. He told Randy his parent's bodies were taken to the nearby funeral home. Randy was devastated by the news but thanked him and told him that he and his brother Karl would be there in a few days.

Once he was off the phone with Sheriff Kane, Randy called Karl and gave him the bad news. After they calmed down, they were able to talk for a while and finally agreed they were going to go up to their parent's home together and take all their heavy-duty hunting rifles with them. Karl told Randy he would pick him up on his way through Portland. They were going to take time off work and stay at their parent's house as long as they had to hunt down and kill the animals that had killed their parents. Randy and Karl were both avid hunters and believed they could hunt down the forest's grizzlies and kill them.

They got to their parent's house in a few days and cleaned up the broken furniture and blood spots on the floors and walls. As they were cleaning it up, Randy said, "This is just sick. I can't believe a couple of grizzly bears did this. Usually, bears stay away from people that are armed with rifles."

Karl replied, "You're right. This looks like it's something else besides bears, but not sure exactly what. Whatever it was, I'm not going to let the animals that did this get away with it."

Zak, Julie, and Seth found out about Don and Gladys and knew what had killed them. They waited a few days, then drove out and met up with Randy and Karl and gave them their condolences. While there, Zak began to tell them about the creatures that the UFO had dropped off, and they were the ones killing all the people in the mountains. Zak told them he believed the creatures did this to their parents. They asked Seth what the creatures looked like, and he said, "They look a lot like a cross between a Grizzly and a Bigfoot, but they're larger, stronger, smarter, and they're pure killers."

Randy told them that he and Karl would go into the forest starting the following day, find and kill the creatures. The three of them had to work but told them where they believed they could find the creatures and explained how to get there. Zak said, "I hope you guys do kill them. We need to get rid of the creatures before they kill everyone that lives up here in this area."

The next day Randy and Karl headed deep into the mountains with their high-powered rifles. They were filled with emotion as they made it deep into the forest. They were going to hunt the creatures like they would hunt deer. They set up a deer stand attached about fifteen feet up in a tree. They had their hiding places about a half-mile apart from each other, along the trail, as they just sat there and waited.

They spent several days waiting to get a shot at the creatures but didn't have any luck. Then on the 6th day, they spotted a Bigfoot just lumbering along the trail, and it didn't seem vicious or threatening. They didn't know it, but it was one of the indigenous Bigfoot that had been in the forest for a long time, and it had never tried to harm a human. Within a hundred and fifty yards of where Randy was perched high in the tree and didn't see him. Randy thought it was one of the creatures that had killed his parents, so he took careful aim and shot right in the middle of its chest. When he did that, the shot rang out, and a small cloud of smoke flew up in the air as he thought the bullet met its target. When Randy looked back down at his target, it was surprisingly gone. It was nowhere to be seen. Randy was sure his bullet hit its mark, but how could he have disappeared so quickly. Randy didn't see him run away. He thought, "Wow. Maybe I missed him, and he ducked behind a tree and into the woods."

Randy was shocked as he climbed to the ground and went looking for the animal. Not finding a dead body, he was confused as to what may have happened. He'd been on a lot of hunts and had killed a lot of smaller animals than this one and from a further distance away, so he believed there was no way he could've missed that large animal as close as he was.

Hearing the gunshot, Karl came running down the trail and met up with Randy. He went up to him, saying, "Did you get it?"

Randy's face was blank and white as he said, "Well, I thought I did, but as soon as I fired my rifle, it disappeared. Man, he must have been quick to avoid that bullet." He and Karl then talked about what Zak had told them regarding the creatures coming out of the UFO, and now they were starting to accept the unbelievable story he had told them. Randy said to Karl, "I don't know what's going on up here, but I think we've been hunting ghosts."

The next day Randy and Karl didn't say anything to anyone as they gave up on their hunt and packed to go back home. Before leaving, they made arrangements for all their parent's animals and boarded up the house.

Zak and Seth talked to them just before they left and asked if they got the creatures. Randy said, "Hell no, but we tried, we got a shot at one of them from a short distance away, but strangely enough, it disappeared as soon as I fired my weapon. We have to leave them up to you guys and get back to our jobs. I don't know what's going around here, but it sure and the hell isn't normal. It's something more than the two of us can solve."

Chapter 20 - Shief Escapes

The allied forces had bombed the Tora Bora region fiercely several times in their effort to terminate the Monster, Shief. Their entail given them not only by Zak, but another well-kept secret informant had assured them that Shief was in that location, and he was identified.

The brass and the CIA didn't know that the well-paid and highly groomed informant was a firmly entrenched Taliban brother. One fighter had worked with Shief and those closes to him for weeks in a plan to scurry shief from that region. They were trying to move him into a safer town on the outer reaches of Syria.

Yes, he was there at Tora Bora but taken from there quickly before the bombardment, which began. Several innocent lives were taken in that barrage, but Shief no more cared about that than the many countless lives he had personally taken.

A long, perilous journey had been undertaken to arrive here at these shores. One mistake, one false betrayal, and he would be ended. But he knew from the moment he left the Tora Bora region that he would not stay in his beloved country or even his sacred brothers' countries.

He was filled with too much hatred and passion for revenge to allow the American, Zak Thomas, "The Monster Hunter" (to live, as the informant told Shief, Zak was called).

Shief scoffed," "The Monster Hunter." "I'll go to America to Washington state, a state named after another misguided fool," Shief thought. "There, I will seek and find my revenge."

On the shore, a boat languished. Its hull softly beat against the subtle waves. A silhouetted figure rose from the water, walked up to the sand, dropped to his knees, and raised his hands to the sky, proclaimed, "Allah Akbar."

A single car sat at the crest of the beachhead. Taking a narrow path to the car, the figure climbed inside next to the driver. "Is everything prepared?" The figure said. "Just as you requested."

A voice from the back seat replied. Many lives were taken, payoffs and bribes were made to ensure that Shief would arrive safely to these Western shores of Gibraltar.

He was the least they could do, being one the most prominent and prolific freedom fighters that the Taliban had created. "You'll be leaving this evening on the freighter to America. With the restrictions that the American Homeland Security has on commercial flights, you're right, it will take longer, but it will be safer," A second voice in the backseat said.

Shief merely nodded, then pulled a cap that had been given him over his eyes and prepared himself for the two-hour drive to the port for his departure.

Chapter 21- Bungee Jumpers

The daily special at Bessie's Diner was the chicken fried steak and eggs, which consisted of fresh chicken fried steak, country potatoes, two eggs, and white gravy poured on top. Zak never cared for it, but sheriff Kane loved it and ordered it at least a couple of times a week.

As they sat at Bessie's counter, the sheriff plowed into a big heaping of gravy on his potatoes. "Zak, I asked you here for two reasons, Kane said in between bites. First, "In light of Daniel's deaths and how it took place, I think you might be on to something, and I apologize from the other day, not listening to you further. But Monsters? I'm not sure I want to commit that far in, but I'll say, I agree, there's something out there that's not right." "More than just bear attacks."

Zak, who had been looking down at the sheriff's plate, could only sit in amazement at how someone could carry on an entire conversation and manage to consume a full plate of chicken-fried steak breakfast. Zak remarked. "Julie, Seth, and I went into those woods, and we saw those creatures ourselves. They killed Ben right in front of us inside the cave. Everything I have been telling you is the truth. That girl Mary that we brought back to town, she'll also verify it, she saw them too, they killed her boyfriend, their nothing but pure killers."

"Yeah, I heard," Kane said, stabbing at a thick piece of steak and sopping it up with the last of his gravy. She told me all about it. I've got an idea of how we can go after these bastards, and I'm going to need your help with it."

"But also, right now, I'm dealing with a different issue that I have to take care of that involves two different bizarre deaths by none other than Bungee Jumpers found up on Sawtooth ridge. You know anything about Bungee Jumping?" Kane asked Zak.

"Not much, seen it at a few fairs, saw it a few times overseas, but you can't bungee jump off that mountain." Zak's mind suddenly flashed back to the horrors he had seen at the hands of Shief.

"Damndest thing about that sport. You would think that the people who do it would have checked and double-checked their line's distance to the ground. But here I have two cases where two of these enthusiasts did not do exactly that. What are the odds." Kane said as he took the last bite of his breakfast. "There's no way I would even think about doing it, jump off a cliff, shitttt, no way."

That brings up another head-scratcher. You know those people that worked and died in the twin towers that came down on 9/11.

"Sure," Zak said. "Why In the hell, if you work on the 90th floor of one of those towers and you're a savvy broker who deals with investments and trading, why you wouldn't have invested into one of those mini parachutes and kept the thing? In your office. If you got stuck in a fire up there, then you jump out the window, and you float down to safety, not one of them did it."

Zak only looked at him blankly and thought, "How the hell does that relate to our problem."

It was only later, when he got home, that he received the message from an old Army buddy that it all became more evident to him. "Shief is here?"

"But how did he survive the blasts from all the bombs that were aimed at him in Tora Bora. All reports said he was killed. If he did survive, what the hell is he doing in my hometown?" Zak whispered. As he lay in bed that night and tried to sleep, a scary thought came to his mind. "What if Shief had somehow survived and then found where I lived and was now stalking me? Maybe he was toying with me by killing the two so-called Bungee Jumpers in the way he did just to let me know he was here. If it is him, he could've killed me any time he wanted." Then he remembered how twisted and sick Shief was and killing the two guys in how he did fit his method of operation. Shivering from the thought, he closed his eyes but didn't get much sleep the rest of that night as he whispered again, "Oh crap, it's got to be him."

Early the following day, Zak headed to Julie's house, and he wanted to catch her before she got to school. He caught her just after she got out of the shower, and she had just gotten dressed and starting on her long blond hair. When she went to the door, she could tell something was wrong because he was pale as a ghost. She said, "Zak, what are you doing here? Is something wrong?"

Zak replied, "Yes, I think I have a huge problem, and it's not the creatures." Julie invited him in and told him to talk to her while she was doing her hair and let her know what was going on.

He began by saying, "You know I've had a hard time talking to you about my time in Afghanistan, and I'm sorry, but right now, I need to tell you everything that I went through over there." She sat in front of the mirror and combed her hair out as she watched him and listened intently to every word, as he told her everything, including the part about him volunteering to hunt down the serial killer Mohammed Shief.

When he was done, she said, "Oh My God, Zak, I had no idea. No wonder you have had such PTSD issues. That's a lot to keep bottled up inside."

Zak said, "That's not the worst part, the monster, Shief didn't die once I had him cornered like everyone thought he did. I don't know how he did it, but I believe he made it out alive."

"Seriously," said Julie.

"Yes, and that's not the worst part, I believe he's hunted down where I live, and now, he's here to kill me."

Julie said, "What? How do you know that?

Sheriff Kane told me about a couple of guys who tried to bungee jump off the top of Sawtooth Ridge. "Nobody in their right minds would ever attempt something that suicidal. It can't be done. He said the jumpers didn't plan out their jump very well because they both jumped at the same time and hit the ground, and they were crushed to death by the rocks below."

Julie's eyes widened as she cupped her mouth with both hands and said, "That's horrible."

Zak said, "That was Shief's exact way of killing people in Afghanistan. He laughed and jumped up and down as he pushed them to their deaths. I believe he killed those two guys to let me know he was here. He was sending me a message to let me know. I believe he is playing a sick and twisted game with me. If he wasn't, all he had to do is hide and wait for me and then kill me. It would've been easy for him."

A wide-eyed Julie asked, "So what are you going to do, Zak?"

He replied, "First of all, I would like for you to go stay with your mother and father for a few weeks until I find this guy and kill him."

Julie said, "What about my job? I can't just get up and take off and leave."

Zak replied, "Believe me, Julie, this guy will use you to get to me. I know him. If you want to keep us both alive, you'll go stay with your parents."

Julie said, "Ok, Zak, whatever you think is best for us. I'll call them and tell them I'm coming, but what about the creatures?"

Zak said I could only deal with one monster at a time, and right now, this one is after me and wants to kill me. I'm going to talk to Seth and come up with some plan to lure him out of hiding and kill him for the last time."

Chapter 22 - The Cat and Mouse Game with Shief

Zak called into work and told them he was sick and wouldn't be coming in for a few weeks. He talked to Seth in length about everything and told him he had to be careful with this guy because he was a true monster, and if he knew anyone was helping him, he would take them captive and torture them before killing them. He told Seth they had to be constantly vigilant because Shief was sneaky dangerous.

Shief was crafty; he had rented a room in a neighboring town just far enough away where Zak would have a hard time knowing where he was. He had plans he was now going to be the hunter instead of the hunted like Zak had done with him in Afghanistan. Once he had Zak where he wanted him, then he would capture and punish him. He already had planned how he would draw Zak out and torture him before he took him up the Ridge and threw him over as he had done with two bungee jumpers. When he was alone in his room, he would think about what he was going to do to Zak. He would get excited and laugh aloud and say, "Soon, my friend, soon!"

He believed it would be easy to get Zak any time he wanted because he knew he had a few weaknesses. One was his wife, Julie, and the other was his cousin Seth. He believed that if he could take one of them captive, Zak would do anything he wanted. Unfortunately for him, when he did that to the two "Bungee Jumpers" at the Ridge, Zak believed it was him or a copy-cat, and it gave him enough warning to remove Julie from the threat.

Believing it may be him, Zak and Seth came up with their own plan to spend all their time together until the psychopath reared his ugly head. The only time we are going to be separated from each other is when we're in the bathroom, so we'll have each other's back." Zak said, "If he follows his M.O. Then he will be like one of the creatures that want to knock me in the head and carry me to the Ridge. Knowing how he thinks he will come after you and Julie to try and get to me. We have to try to think like him and stay one step ahead of him."

They went on their offensive and started searching for Shief. They knew he was hiding out someplace in the area; they just didn't know where. Their first stop was to talk to Sheriff Kane and tell him to be on the look-out for a foreigner with a strong accent, that may be asking questions about Zak. Zak told him the guy they were looking for was a killer from Afghanistan that had killed many American Soldiers and had to be stopped. He told Kane the crazed killer wanted to kill him now.

Kane said, "Man, you sure get yourself into some shit, Zak!"

Zak said, "I know, Sheriff, I can't help it."

They talked to their friends in town and at work and told them to keep an eye out for any suspicious man asking questions about Zak. They put up signs to try and intimidate Shief that said, "I know you're here, come and get me." They were trying to make him angry enough to draw him out into the open.

When he saw the signs, he was cool as a cucumber, lying low and not falling for any of their tricks that may hit a nerve with him. When he saw their signs, he laughed and whispered, "Clever, my friend, very clever."

Zak figured he'd come after Seth soon, so they purchased night scopes for their rifles and decided to take a hiding place up in the trees and the woods just outside Seth's house. They were each about fifteen feet off the ground and perched on a deer stand just waiting for Shief. They were about seventy-five yards apart from each other as they waited patiently. They left the lights on in the living room and an outside porch light on to lure Shief in. They believed he'd come and try and take Seth while he was sleeping and use him as his pawn.

They waited for the next three nights, and nothing happened until the fourth night when the monster went for the bait. It was around three in the morning when Zak and Seth watched as the armed figure carefully crept up to the house. He kept a low profile as he approached the porch and slowly moved to the window and looked inside. He went over to the front door and tried to turn the knob. Surprisingly, he thought, "It's not locked." Then he realized he had been set up. Just as he quickly turned around to run, a shot rang out from Zak's rifle, and the stalker went down. He rolled around for a few seconds and then got back to his feet and took off running into the woods and disappeared. Zak and Seth fired several more shots at him, but they missed their target.

Zak and Seth carefully climbed out of their hiding place and methodically approached the porch. Seth looked down on the porch floor and said, "You got him; there's blood here."

Zak replied, "Yeah, but he got away again."

They went to Zak's house and took turns and got a little sleep as Shief made it back to his hotel room. He was pissed and shouting in Arabic as he threw the door open and went inside. "I can't believe I let that bastard shoot me. I should've known."

He had been shot in the left shoulder, and the bullet went clean through, but he'd lost a lot of blood. Once inside, he quickly grabbed a towel, put pressure on the wound, and fetched his first aid kit. He gritted his teeth as he sewed the wound up, cursing the entire time. "You got me this time, you son of a bitch, but it won't happen again. I should've just killed you instead of playing the stupid game with you." Then he thought for a moment and laughed as he said, "Na, what fun would that be?"

The next day Zak and Seth checked the local doctor's offices to see if anyone had come in with a bullet wound. There wasn't any report by any doctors or hospitals, so Zak said, "Now he's going to be out for blood. He'll be like a wounded grizzly bear and won't stop until he finds me."

Zak softly whispered, "Maybe we should lure him back into the woods and have him follow us up to where the creatures are staying in the underground cave. Let's give him a few days to recuperate from his flesh wound, and then we'll use me as bait."

Seth replied, "What happens if the creatures go after you and try to kill you instead of him?"

Zak replied, "To be honest, I'm not sure which one of the monsters I'm most afraid of encountering. They're all evil killers."

Zak and Seth started spreading the word to everyone in town that they would go out in the woods on Thursday and hunt for the creatures. They had a few volunteers that wanted to go with them, but Zak politely turned them down as he said, "Thank you, but no, not on this hunt. Seth and I have to do this one alone."

Their plan worked, and Shief had gotten the news. He figured it would be the perfect time to put his plan in place. Before they were ready to disappear into the woods, Zak instantly recognized the person he had so desperately pursued in Afghanistan. He was about two hundred yards from them and armed with a rifle. He was standing watching as he gave Zak a salute just before he went into the woods. "Zak thought, "That is one crazy and fearless son of a bitch. He's got a lot of guts standing there with an automatic rifle over his shoulder." Zak knew that if he turned around and went after him, he would disappear before he got close to him, so he had to follow his plan.

Just before they went into the woods, Zak told Seth, "You hang back until he makes it into the woods, and he's on my trail, and then you come in behind him and stay a few hundred yards back. Be careful he doesn't backtrack on you because he's good at that. Keep your eyes open for the creatures, too, because they're out there, somewhere doing their hunting. I don't want anything to happen to you trying to get his bastard."

Zak was hiking along the trail, and Shief was following in pursuit, being too focused on Zak to pay attention to Seth. He reacted just like Zak figured he would as they moved along at a brisk pace for a few hours and made it almost to the cave opening. Shief had his plan on how he was going to kill Zak. At one point near some high brush along the trail, Seth lost sight of Shief, and he was gone. He had left the trail and started to circle in the woods to get ahead of Zak. Once in place, he would surprise Zak when he jumped out in front of him with weapons drawn and take him captive or kill him.

When he got off the trail and in the thick brush, he was in unfamiliar territory, and movement through the woods was slow and restricted. He then realized his plan to get ahead of Zak would never work. He headed back in the direction of the trail and found his way back onto it after several minutes. Seth sat in the same position, watching and waiting to see if Shief would show up again, and he did. He headed in Zak's direction once again, with Seth not far behind.

Once near the cave opening, Zak came to an abrupt stop and turned around, and faced Shief. He was about one hundred and fifty yards from Zak but seeing what he had done, Shief also came to a stop. Seth continued sneaking closer to Shief.

Zak was acting submissive as he began yelling back down to Shief, "Ok, you got me, you win."

Shief let out a laugh and said, "Just like that, you're giving up? But you need to take the dive over the cliff."

Zak joked with him and said, "Well, how about you go first, and I watch." He was killing time just waiting for Seth to get into a shooting position about a hundred yards away from Shief.

Shief laughed aloud and said, "That's not what I had planned, my friend."

Zak thought, "My Friend, I'm not his friend. I hate this guy! He's a complete whack job, a sicko, and a ruthless killer." Then one of the creatures let out one of its massive cries, and it wasn't too far away.

Shief said, "What was that, one of your pets?" as he laughed aloud again.

Then the shot rang out from Seth's rifle, and it hit Shief in the upper left thigh. He instantly tried to get to his feet when Seth reshot him in the other thigh. Now he was unable to walk at all with two shattered legs; he could only crawl. He was not giving up easily as he tried to aim at Zak with his rifle as he lay on the ground. Zak then shot him in his shooting arm, and the rifle went flying in the air and landed several feet away. Zak slowly walked over to him and said, "You should've died at Tora Bora Shief. It's no place for you to be eaten by creatures in the woods. You should've let it go and just stayed dead."

Shief replied, "What do you mean creatures; you're the only creature I see? Besides, you are still here. I couldn't just let it go. You hunted me like a wild animal in my country. You made my life miserable, always trying to kill me."

Zak mocked him and said, "You'll soon get your just rewards for all your evil deeds, "My Friend!""

Zak and Seth gathered up Shief's weapons, and Zak gave him a half salute as they headed back down the trail. Shief was saying, "Hey, you can't just leave me out here; there are bears out here, they'll eat me."

Zak turned around and said, "That's exactly what they'll do, but they're not bears."

They left him there and went about fifty yards down the path, then Zak turned to Seth and said, "Hold up," and turned back toward Shief. Approaching him again, Zak said, "I'm not a monster like you," And Zak stared at Shief for a moment.
"No, you're the monster hunter!" Shief laughed as he grimaced from his pain. If he was not such a ruthless killer, Zak might have had a lot of respect for his tenacity.

Raising his rifle, Zak said, "I can't leave you again without knowing you're not dead, "Wild Dog." Shief looked up at him, and an echoing shot rang out, and Shief's head jerked backward, and his lifeless body slumped sideways.

Zak leaned forward and placed his hand on Seth's shoulder as he said to Seth, "We got rid of one monster today. We will come back soon and get the other two. But right now, let's get the hell out of here so I can call Julie and let her know she's safe."

Chapter 23 - It is Not Funny

Miles from the nearest town, there is a lonely dirt road that winds down into the Skokomish wilderness's southeastern part. The one-lane dirt and pebble road has thick and overhanging trees covering the entire road like a dome. There are potholes that even a four-wheel vehicle has to dodge and weave that has been there for years.

It is dark and intimidating, especially when the sun starts to go down at night. Before the creatures had started killing people in the forest, Zak had a couple of friends that told him they had gone up the road to do a little deer hunting one day. They hunted too long, and it was almost dark by the time they were on their way home. Their pick-up hit a pothole in the road, and it knocked a hole in their gas tank. They didn't get far before the truck ran out of gas.

One of the friends told the other to stay in the vehicle, and he would get help. Even though the other friend had a rifle with him, he said, "Don't leave me here alone. I'll be dead by the time you get back. If the wild animals don't get me, I'll shoot myself because of my fear." When Zak heard that story, he couldn't help but laugh as he said, "I know that road, and it's scary as hell, so what did you do?" His friend chuckled and said, "We both went to get help together."

The road is snowed in for a few months a year and not assessable during the deep winter. Several old wooden cabins have been there for over two hundred years, and one of Zak's older cousins, Clifford, had lived in one of the old houses for years with his wife and two teenage daughters. He didn't seem to be much afraid of anything because he'd seen all kinds of wild animals in the woods throughout the years, but nothing that ever scared him.

Not too long after, all the stories about the two creatures Seth and Zak had seen started circulating town. Clifford heard about them and called Zak and asked him if he, Julie, and Seth could come for a BBQ on Saturday. Zak felt like he needed to break from the creatures and thought it would be a perfect time to do it. He talked to Julie and Seth, and they agreed to go.

They were having a good time visiting Clifford and his family. It had just gotten dark, and they were all sitting at a patio table outside and relaxing after dinner when Clifford's wife began to tell them about a strange experience their family had just a few weeks earlier. She seemed a little scared to even talk about it.

As she told them what happened, she said, "We were all asleep, and it was the middle of the night when we heard something that was across the dirt road and in the woods. At first, we thought there was a woman and a baby in the woods because we thought we heard a baby crying. Then we heard it start saying Mama, Mama, over and over again. It was the craziest thing hearing that baby in the woods. It was loud enough to wake all of us up and go to the back door to see what it was. We were all standing outside and trying to figure out what it could be. We thought, could it really be a baby out in the woods looking for its Mama?"

Zak, Seth, and Julie were so enthralled in the story that they didn't pay any attention as the oldest daughter got up from the table and went into the house. Clifford's wife continued to tell them that Clifford and the oldest daughter each grabbed a rifle and started to cross the dirt road next to the house to find the crying baby. "There was no moon out, and it was extra dark and scary that night. It was just the creepiest thing we'd ever heard in the woods as it continued to keep saying in a pitiful and painful voice, Mama, Mama, Mama. As soon as they went across the dirt road and near the woods, the voice stopped. There was a strange odor in the air. It smelled like a dead animal. They shined their flashlight in all directions, but there was nothing to be seen. Whatever it was almost instantly disappeared once they shined their lights around. We didn't get much sleep the rest of the night because whatever it was made us all feel uneasy."

Just as she finished up her story, the oldest daughter had gone inside and put on a guerilla suit, and just when her mom had everyone's attention. She snuck up behind the corner of the house, jumped out, raised her arms in the air, and let out a deep human growl. Seth was so into the story that when she jumped out, it startled him, and he yelled out, "What the hell," and ran over a couple of chairs and a table trying to get away from her. Julie screamed, and Zak stood up and took a defensive fighting posture. The two daughters got a big laugh out of it as she pulled off the mask and said, "We got you."

Julie thought it was a little bit too much considering what was going on with the creatures. Zak was a little angry at first because he felt like they were taking the stories about the creature too lightly and making fun of them. He said in a deep stern voice, "Everything you've heard about the creatures is true. It's no laughing matter. Those creatures are killing people around here. You better keep an eye out for them because you never know where they will strike next. They could come after your entire family."

Clifford's wife said, "Oh. My God, Zak. I hope not."

A little later, as they were leaving, Clifford pulled Zak aside and whispered, "I'm sorry about the bad prank the girls pulled on you guys, but everything about that story is true. It really happened."

Chapter 24 – Fishing the Skokomish River

It was the end of May, and school had just gotten out for fifteen-year-old Josh Gibbins. He had just finished his second year of high school. He lived in Hoodsport, and his father Fredrick had promised him that he would take him fishing for Steelhead off the banks of the Skokomish River as soon as school was out.

Josh had been looking forward to this day for a long time because fishing was his favorite thing he loved to do. They got up at four in the morning, and his mom Trudy had already prepared them each packed lunch in a picnic basket. She had it sitting on the kitchen table along with a small ice chest filled with their favorite soft drinks and packed in ice. Josh thanked his mom for everything as he took them to the pick-up.

Josh didn't get much sleep that night as he oiled his reel and checked the pole several times to make sure everything was set precisely right. He had a hard time sleeping that night because he was worried. He was going to forget something he needed. He was so paranoid about it that he rechecked everything before they left. He put the rod and reels in the bed of the pick-up, then yelled to his father, "Hey dad, I got everything in the pick-up, so whenever you're ready, I am too."

His dad replied, "Ok, I'm going to grab my coat and the rifle, and then I'll be ready to go."

Josh wondered, "We're just going fishing, no need for a gun, but again, there were a lot of bears in that part of the country." Fredrick kissed Trudy and told her they would be back sometime near or right after dark.

They were both a little sleepy from getting up so early and didn't talk much on the way to the banks of the Skokomish River. Josh was thinking about that big one he wanted to land. They got there just as the sun was starting to come up. Fredrick parked the pick-up near the river as he could get, but it was still about forty yards away. He told Josh to stick the picnic basket and ice chest in the truck's cab so the bears and other animals would leave it alone. He didn't lock the truck because they were going to be fishing not far away.

Josh's hands were shaking because he was so excited about catching that first big fish. His dad said, "Slow down, Josh. Those fish aren't going to go anywhere."

Josh replied, "I know, dad, but I want to get the first fish before you."

Fredrick laughed and said, "Ha, ha, fat chance! Good luck with that!"

They were having a lot of luck bringing them in, and Josh landed the first one that was seventeen inches and weighed about four pounds and another that was just a little larger. He looked over at his dad and smiled. His dad caught a couple, and they were having a lot of fun landing the beauties. It was just what Josh was hoping.

They hadn't been paying much attention to anything around them because they were so busy catching fish when suddenly someone or something threw a large rock into the water, not too far from where they were fishing. It was a little larger than a grapefruit, and Fredrick said, "What the hell was that?" He thought, "What could throw a rock that size from over there in the woods?" He and Josh began looking around, and then another large rock was thrown not too far from them once again. Josh started to get angry because he felt like whoever was doing that would scare the fish away. Josh looked over at his dad and said, "Hey Dad, what's up with that? Someone is trying to ruin our fishing spot?"

He could see that his dad was a little rattled as he said, "I don't know, but I think we better pack up our things and get out of here as soon as we can."

Josh didn't waste any time because he could see the fear in his dad's face. He had his things in his hands and ready to go as he started walking briskly toward the pick-up. The massive male creature stepped out from behind a large bush where it had been hiding and stood up. It was only about fifteen feet away from Fredrick when it let out one of its bellowing screams. Shocked by the scream and the massive size of the creature, Fredrick said, "Oh crap, run for the truck Josh and get the gun." Josh turned around and got a brief look at the creature and then dropped his gear and took off running as fast as he could go. He believed his dad was right behind him. Once he got inside the truck, he grabbed the rifle and looked back for his dad, but he was nowhere to be seen. He was gone.

Josh was shaking uncontrollably and trying to load the rifle while he was saying, "Come on, come on, get this thing loaded." He had the rifle pointed out in front of him as he slowly got out of the truck and made his way to where he last saw his dad standing in front of the creature. When he got to the spot, there was no sign of his dad or the creature. Josh searched up and down the river for his dad, but he was gone. Josh couldn't believe that maybe the creature had taken him. The only thing left of his dad was his dad's fishing pole and gear lying in the sand where he had disappeared. He checked for his cell phone, but he had forgotten it in his hurry to leave the house that morning. He yelled out, "Shit, shit, shit, what do I do now?" He thought, "Maybe I should wait here for a while and see if dad shows up." He waited for a few hours, and there was no sign of his dad or the creature. The entire time, he was looking all around to make sure the creature wasn't coming after him.

It was the middle of the afternoon, and he knew he didn't want to be out there alone when it got dark. He had to do something.

Fredrick always kept a spare key taped to a wheel bar above the front left tire, and Josh knew where it was. He went as fast as he could, but he was scared and shaking uncontrollably as he retrieved the key.

When he started up the truck, he had tears in his eyes as he quickly drove out of the area and onto the main road. He was feeling lucky that his dad had recently taught him how to drive. He felt like it was the emptiest feeling he'd ever had in his life as he pulled away from the fishing hole. He went to the nearest town and then was able to call his mom and let her know what happened. The first thing he said to her over the phone as he cried out was, "A Bigfoot creature got dad."

Chapter 25 - Hunt for Fredrick

A few hours later, after not seeing Fredrick walk through the door, the distraught Trudy contacted the local Deputy Sheriff Walter Calhoun from the neighboring town where her husband went missing. The Deputy asked if Josh could come and show him where he had been fishing when his dad disappeared.

When they got to his office, he had them jump in his patrol car so they could go out to the scene where the abduction took place. On the way, Calhoun asked Josh questions about the fishing trip and exactly what happened. He asked Josh if he got a look at the animal, he believed, took his dad. Josh said that he did get a brief look at it when he turned to look back at his dad. He told him it was right after the animal screamed and right after his dad told him to run to the truck.

He said the animal looked like it was moving aggressively toward his dad and only a few feet away from him. He said it was tall and massive, maybe around eight or nine feet, and looked like a Bigfoot. The deputy asked him what it looked like, and Josh said, "It was the creepiest looking thing I've ever seen; it looked a little like a bear, but more like a human, and the sound it made was creepy and scary."

Wanting to know where her husband was last seen and to give Josh moral support, Trudy rode quietly in the back seat, and the tears started swelling up in her eyes when Josh talked about the animal and his dad. She had a handkerchief in her hand and was occasionally wiping the dripping tears from her face.

Josh was a little reluctant to go back to the location, but in his heart, he was holding out some small hope his dad would be waiting for them when they got there. Unfortunately, when they arrived at the fishing hole, he was not there. To josh, it felt quiet and dark, not the happy place it had been earlier. As they approached, he thought, "I'll never go fishing again."

Once there, Josh and Calhoun got out of the vehicle, and Josh stood close by the door. He told Calhoun that was as far as he was going to go. He did not have a weapon and wasn't going to take any chances, just if the creature was still around. Calhoun walked up and down the riverbank until he came across the footprints of the creature. He found Josh and Fredrick's fishing gear near the river, where they had dropped them. He made a call to his office so they could have someone come out and take an imprint of the giant footprints.

He went over and talked to Josh and his mother and said, "You're right, Josh, I found some huge footprints, and that thing is big, and it's not a bear. The footprints are different than that of a bear's paw." They waited about thirty minutes for one of his office staff to arrive to get the plaster print of the footprints. Josh was uncomfortable the entire time they were there, feeling like he was on pins and needles for fear of the creature returning.

Once his staff arrived, Calhoun told them to start putting together a search party to look for Fredrick and the creature. "Tell everyone to be well-armed; I don't know what we're dealing with here. Tell them we'll head up into the forest tomorrow morning and see what we can find."

"Ok, Sir, I'll get it all set up," They spent just a little longer and then headed back to town.

Josh asked the deputy, "I have a rifle, so is it ok if I go with you tomorrow and search for my dad?" He looked over at Trudy, and she shook her head that it was okay with her. She said, "If you can protect him from the huge animal, it will be okay with me. I don't want to lose him too by whatever this thing is."

He said, "I will, Ma'am, but he'll have to be at my office about five in the morning and ready to go." She said, "He will. I'll make sure he's on time, Deputy." She knew Josh had to do this and didn't try to fight him or stop him.

The following day Josh joined up with twelve other hunters, including Calhoun. Before they left, Calhoun talked to everyone and said, "I don't know what we're dealing with out there, so let's be alert." He looked over at Josh and said, "This thing is big and has already taken one man we know about, and it's probably what has been taking the hikers and killed Don and Gladys Daniels. I believe it's probably hiding out around the caves somewhere, so we'll head up in that direction. "Josh was nervous as the group headed into the forest, but he was holding out hope his dad may still be found alive. He thought, "Maybe we can find out, one way or another, if he's dead or alive."

The creatures were becoming intuitive; they had been in the forest for about a month now. They were used to the animal and the bird sounds in the woods. They could tell from the different sounds they made when a human was getting close, and they could tell if a person was alone or with a group. They could choose the human prey they felt was the most vulnerable, just like Fredrick. He was away from his truck and didn't have a weapon on him when he was taken. In the case of a large group that was all armed, the creatures could watch them from a distance, or they could go deep into the caves and hide from them. They were smart enough to know when to abduct someone or not and when to kill someone or not.

As the group made their way deeper into the forest, the darker and creeper it became. At the base of Sawtooth Ridge, the deputy said, "Ok, let's spread out about fifteen to twenty feet apart and sweep this area." Once off the trail, it was slow going, but they dredged on. As they got nearer to the caves, the creatures began to let out their screams. Everyone started saying, "Hey, what the hell was that."

Josh yelled out, "That's the creature that took my dad. That's the scream they make."

It was getting around lunchtime, and they had been walking for about four hours and not able to see the creatures when Calhoun said, "Ok, let's take a break and grab something to eat." Everyone had packed a lunch, and Trudy had made one for Josh.

After a quick lunch, one of the hunters said, "I need to go to the bathroom." He had a used roll of toilet paper in his left hand as he took off about forty yards away from the rest of the group and into the thick woods. Just as he got to the spot he had chosen, he let out a blood-curdling scream as the large male creature swooped in on him and scooped him up. When he screamed, the killer instantly snapped his neck and then headed deeper into the forest with his latest kill over his shoulders.

By the time Calhoun and the men got there, all they found was the roll of toilet paper lying on the ground, and the hunter was nowhere to be found. They quickly spread out, searching for the hunter and any sign of the creature, but there was nothing. They spent about two hours searching the area for the hunter before giving up. Not finding any sign of him, Calhoun said, "We have to get out of this forest because if that creature can take one of us that fast and easy, it could get all of us, one at a time, before we could make it out of here before dark. We're going to need a lot more help hunting this creature."

Josh was disheartened by giving up the hunt for his dad, but now, he realized that his dad was dead like the hunter.

Chapter 26 - Josh Wants Revenge

Josh went back home after the search and told his mom what happened to the hunter and that they couldn't find any sign of him or his dad. He would be out of school for a few months and knew he had nothing but time on his hands to relive what happened that day on the riverbank. He kept going over it repeatedly in his mind, thinking he could've done something to help his dad, but he felt a little guilty because he ran and left his dad alone with the creature.

He could feel the anger in his body building toward the creature, as he thought about it, so much that he was becoming obsessed with his thoughts of revenge. He isolated himself in his room and sat by the open window, and stared out for hours. At night he listened to the crickets and envisioned what he wanted to do to the creature he had seen take his dad. He wanted to kill it and tear its heart out as it had done to him and his mom.

After constantly dwelling on it for a few weeks, he didn't tell his mom, but he had made plans with a friend and his dad to take him to the edge of the forest and drop him off. He was armed with his dad's high-powered hunting rifle, extra ammunition, and a sharp skinning knife.

When they arrived where his dad went missing, the sun was coming up, but it was pitch black when he looked toward the tree line. As his friend and his dad left, he thanked them for giving him a ride. As he walked into the woods, nothing, not a sound from anything, and it was creepy quiet. He stopped for a minute and listened to it, the darkness that was ahead of him. Now his brain started to tell him what his heart didn't want to admit; he was suddenly terrified.

Not giving in to his fears, he dredged a little deeper into the forest. He moved slowly, with his rifle in both hands, like he was hunting for a deer. The deeper he went into the woods, the eerier the feelings of not alone growing stronger. It appears someone or something was watching him, and he had a sense of impending doom. He whispered, "Don't kill me."

Once again, he ignored the feeling and dredged forward. When he got close to Sawtooth Ridge, it was mid-morning, and now, he heard something in the woods, and it was just far enough out past the tree line that he couldn't see it because of the thick brush. Then suddenly, a stick came flying in his direction. It landed only a few feet from him, and so now he knew he didn't just imagine things. He wasn't alone. He strained his eyes to see if he could get a glimpse of what threw the stick but couldn't.

He continued slowly along the trail when he heard something that was only 20 to 30 yards in front of him and on both sides of the trail. Then now, a large limb was thrown in his direction from just inside the tree line. Then the creatures began to chatter and make whistling sounds like they didn't want him there. It startled Josh, and he readied his rifle as he whispered, "I'm not leaving this place until you come out in the open." And then he yelled out, "Come and get me, you, coward. I'll blow your head off." The creatures started making growling sounds, and then it screamed that familiar deep, bellowing scream Josh had heard before. It was so close that Josh could smell it, but he felt like the creature was toying with him.

Suddenly, it stepped out from behind a tree and briefly stood there, just looking at him. Josh believed it was the same creature that had taken his dad, so he quickly fired, and as quick as he had pointed his rifle at it, the creature was already behind some thick brush. It took off running, and Josh fired two more shots in its direction. It sounded as though it was crashing through the trees and brush when it let out another scream. It was now pissed that he shot at it.

Zak and Seth had gone into the woods that day and were also hunting the creatures. They were only about a half-mile from Josh when he fired on the creature. They stopped, and Zak said, "Sounds like we have company. Let's go check it out but be careful. We don't want them mistaking us for the creatures and shooting one of us. Seth nodded his head up and down in the agreement, and they picked up their pace until they were able to spot Josh on the trail ahead of them.

As they got closer, Zak yelled out, "Hey, wait up." Josh heard him and immediately turned around and pointed his rifle in their direction. Zak could tell he was a young guy and said, "Hey, take it easy; we're on your side." When he said that, Josh pointed his rifle in another direction and waited for them to approach.

When they got close enough, they were standing only about twenty feet from each other, and Zak said, "What are you doing out here? Are you hunting a deer or what?"

Josh quickly spoke up and said, "No, I'm hunting for the creature that took my dad while we were fishing over at Skokomish River. I just took a few shots at him, and he took off running. I don't think I hit him, but I think I made him angry. I'm going after him right now, and I'm going to kill him."

Zak could see there was no point in trying to talk him out of what he intended as he looked over at Seth and said to Josh, "Did you know there are two of the creatures out here, and you're lucky they haven't killed you?"

Josh was a little surprised when Zak told him there were two of them. He said, "Then I'll kill them both."

Zak replied, "That's what we're doing out here. We've been hunting them for a while, and we want to kill them too. You might as well team up with us, and we can help protect each other as we go after those killers?"

Josh was happy to have help, and the company, as he said, "Sounds good, "They're right up ahead of us." They continued deeper into the forest as Josh told them everything about what happened with his dad.

They were on the trail of the creatures, and they were moving toward their hiding place. They showed themselves a couple more times, but they were a long distance away as the three of them opened fire on them. They continued to take long shots in the creature's direction as they drove them deeper into the forest. Zak wanted the creatures to know that there were people in the woods that would not sit by and let them continue to kill people.

The guys followed them to their underground cave, where they disappeared. Once inside the three of them, they fired several bullets down into the cave entrance to frighten the creatures. They could hear the screams of the creatures deep in the cave. They waited several minutes and then fired down into the cave again.

On the way back, Zak said, "When we get back, I'll give you a ride home, Josh."

He was disappointed that he didn't kill the creature as he was hoping, but he said, "Ok, I appreciate that, but I'm not going to give up on trying to kill those things."

Zak said, "That's fine, but don't go back into those woods without calling us first. If you want to go after them, then let's all go together."

Josh replied, "Ok, I will, I promise."

Chapter 27 - Mom

Jack looked at sheriff Kane's car coming up the driveway and felt a moment of apprehension and puzzlement. Why would he be paying this visit to him and his mom today, and at this late hour in the day, does this guy ever quit.

As sheriff Kane stopped his car and climbed out, Jack immediately said. Ok, ok, Sheriff, I know, I know, mom called you guys again, and it's a false alarm, but she gets scared, and I've talked to her over and over about that darn phone. I'm even thinking of taking the house phone and hiding it where she can't get to it.

Jack's mom was 91 years old and had lived alone in the old family country home that sat on the outer edge of The Skokomish wilderness since Jack's father had passed five years earlier.

Sheriff Kane smiled as he stepped into the yard and said, "Yeah, she can be a real pain in the butt," "But (his expression turned serious), I didn't drive out here for that. No, Jack, I've got something far more pressing."

Jack motioned the sheriff over to a picnic table near the porch and, taking a seat, "Jack, there's a real problem with a couple of, ah, bears that are terrorizing the upper and lower areas of the wilderness that I need to fill you in on, Kane said, as he propped his foot on the seat of the table. Jack stood and waited. "You see, these Bears are not like other bears. They're smarter than your average bear. They're downright crafty," Kane said, as he went on to explain how several people had been killed and even taken by the beasts.

"What do you recommend I do?" Jack said. Well, I know your mom's elderly, and she is not easily transported, and you want to keep her home and not put her in one of those institutions. Keep those doors locked up and keep checking on your mom constantly, and if you have a rifle, keep it handy."

"Will do." Jack thanked him for the heads up. The sheriff waved bye as his tires spun out of the gravel driveway.

Jack had heard the stories circulating about the rogue bears and missing persons as of late, but they had fought off wildlife in the past. Back in the days when he had lived at home with his mom and dad. Even a few minor incidents after his dad had died, and he stayed with his mom for months on end.

However, after retiring from Mountain Cascade Construction Company, he preferred living on his own, closer to town. He still checked on his mom every day but rarely stayed through the night anymore.

He walked into his childhood home and instantly felt at ease; he knew every inch of it. His mom Lois sat on the newer love seat Jack had recently bought for her in Seattle. Lois, at 91, was a frail, short woman weakened by age, blind in one eye and nearly blind in the other, weighing less than 95 pounds. But Jack couldn't and wouldn't put her in a convalescent home unless it became absolutely necessary.

"Bye, Mom, I gotta go now. I'm locking the doors, and I'll check back on you tomorrow."

"Bye, son, I love you so much. You're so handsome," She gushed.

"Yeah, like you can really see me, mom," Jack said while smiling.

After Jack had left, Lois moved toward the kitchen and grabbed a piece of the fried chicken Jack had left for her in the refrigerator. "My good son," Lois softly said.

When Lois felt ready for bed, she always opened her front door for a few minutes and stepped onto the porch to feel the northerly breeze that would rush into her door from the forested hills facing their home. Taking a deep breath, she stepped back inside and closed the house door behind her. As of late, mom was becoming forgetful and confused. As she felt her way to her bedroom, she undressed and changed into her loose-fitting nightgown, slipped into bed, and quickly fell to sleep.

Lois was abruptly woken by the sound of five small bells that Jack had installed on her door to alert her of anyone coming through her front door. Lois sat slightly up in her bed and called out "Jack" (pause) "Jack," A little louder with as much strength as her voice could muster. His footsteps moved forward, and he stood by her bed. "Jack, I'm scared, Jack." (no response) Lois's eyes, blinded by age, looked around and gazed up, "I'm scared by people. I'm scared that someone is going to break in and kill me."

The male creature looking down at the frail older woman, bent down and lightly sniffed her. "JACK, YOU NEED A BATH," Lois exclaimed.

The creature seeing the small female, old and with little weight, posed no threat or benefit to him, straightened up and turned to walk out of the front door toward the waiting woods.

Chapter 28 - Face to Face

Phone in one hand and driving with the other, Sheriff Kane said, "Hello, yes, this is Sheriff Kane, what can I do for you?"

The caller on the other end was a little frantic as he said, "Hey Sheriff, this is Chuck Masters."

Interrupting him, Kane said, "Oh, hey Chuck, I haven't heard from you in a while. What's up?"

Chuck's voice was a little excited and raised as he said, "Things are good with me, but we have a problem out here off of Old Creek Road."

"So, what's the problem?" the Sheriff asked. Chuck said,

"There's a couple of poachers out here, and they were shooting at a deer from their pick-up truck. I'm fairly sure they killed one."

Kane asked, "So did you get a look at them and what they were driving?"

Chuck replied, "Yes, there are two young guys, and they're driving a later model, dark blue, beat up, Ford 150. You can't miss it."

Kane thanked him and said he would talk to him later, as he hung up the phone. "Damn Poachers, this is not deer season, and besides, you can't hunt from the road. They have to know better than that; they'll be in big trouble when I get out there."

He turned on his flashing lights and sped off in that direction. He was angry and mumbling to himself while he was driving. He was driving a little faster than he should, but he wanted to get out there before the poachers had the deer in the back of their pick-up and were gone before he got there. He figured he had a lot of better things to do than to deal with these two idiots right now. He was frustrated and cursing the entire time he was on his way there.

When he got on Old Creek Road, it was just a single-lane dirt road that led deeper into the forest. Loggers once used it to get in and out of the forest. He was throwing up dirt, gravel, and dust as he speeded even faster up the road toward the poachers.

He came to bend in the road, and just as he was coming out of the turn, the male creature ran in front of his patrol car. He immediately slammed on the brakes, and the vehicle slid on the road to a stop as he missed the creature. By then, the female creature was in the middle of the road and right in front of his bumper. She turned her head and shoulder and looked directly at Sheriff Kane. She opened her mouth wide and exposed her long white fangs. For a brief second, they locked eyes with each other, and Kane yelled out, "What the hell?" As he sat there and watched, the female turned back toward the tree line. The male was now waiting for her and started running in that direction once again. The male creature let out a loud, bellowing scream that Sheriff Kane had never heard before.

Once they were out of sight, he just sat there in his patrol car for the longest time and tried to figure out what he had just seen. He knew it was not a bear, but it didn't look like all the reports of sightings of Bigfoot he'd heard about either. He didn't know what they were, but they did have a slightly protruding muzzle like a bear, but it wasn't a bear. It did resemble a human, but it wasn't human. He was confused by their appearance.

As he sat in his patrol car trying to make sense of his encounter, he realized that maybe everything that Zak, Julie, and Seth, had been trying to tell him about the creatures might be true. They looked exactly like what they had described to him, abducting and killing people out in the woods. Even Don Daniels had told him that what he saw in his yard was no bear. Coming to terms with it, he looked at himself in his rear-view mirror and said, "You big stupid dummy, Zak was right."

He had almost forgotten about the poachers because now he was dealing with a problem that he realized was a hell of a lot more dangerous and important than two poachers. Once he collected himself, he gunned his cruiser up around the next bend, and there were the poachers. They were less than a half-mile from where the creatures had crossed the road and freaked out to see him.

Kane figured the creatures were probably after these two guys, so when he saw them, he said, "You two broke the law by killing that deer, but it's your lucky day. I'm going to let you go. But you have to get the hell out of here right now because there are man-eating killers on the loose up here in these woods, and if you're not careful, you'll be their next meal."

Chapter 29 - Creatures Move North

The creatures realized they were now continually hunted by the people from the nearby towns of the Skokomish Wilderness. Fearing they may be shot and killed, they decided to leave the area and find another place to live and hunt for food. They decided to follow the underground cave system north through Brothers Wilderness and Buckhorn Wilderness until they felt comfortable resurfacing in a new location. It took them five days of continuous walking to get to the cave exit in the northeastern part of Buckhorn Wilderness.

The cave system was little known and explored by humans and 200 and 300 feet underground with miles of passageways, steep hills, and open spaces carved out by geological forces. Temperature deep in the cave was always between 50 and 60 degrees, and the totality of darkness is absolute. The creatures were able to find their way through the cave system with their infrared type vision.

One of the cave exits was located at the edge of the Quinault Rain Forrest. That was where the creatures decided to surface once again. It was just beginning to get daybreak when they emerged, and they were hungry and needed to feed. There was still an abundance of wildlife in that part of the forest that hadn't been frightened away so soon they would be feasting in a fresh kill.

Even though the creatures loved the taste of human flesh, they would settle for a good size mule deer right now. As they left the cave, they methodically split up from each other and started hunting for their prey. It was only a short time when the female creature spotted a lone mule deer grazing in a small open meadow area. She whistled to the male with a high pitch shrill sound, and he responded with his return whistle. The deer temporarily looked up from eating and looked around to see where the sound was coming.

The female creature moved slowly around behind the deer and waited for the male creature to move into position. They had the areas covered where the deer may try to escape if it spotted one of them and started to run. They started slowly closing in from the two sides, and when the male was within 20 feet of the deer, the female creature let out a little louder whistle. The deer immediately looked up in fear with its big dark eyes in the direction of the sound. The male was crouched behind some brush, and his eyes were glued on the deer. Once the deer's head was turned and focused on the female creature, the male swiftly took a couple of steps and then lunged on the deer. It happened with such lightning speed the deer didn't have much time to react.

Once the deer was dead, the two creatures teamed up together, and the female looked at the male as if she were very pleased with their kill, and it appeared she had a slight smile on her face. The male threw the deer over his shoulder, and the two of them headed back to the cave. Once inside their new hideout, and because it had been several days from the time they had last eaten, they devoured a lot of the deer in a short period of time. They ripped the meat from the bone with their razer like fangs. The meal would last them a couple of days until they could get used to their new surroundings while exploring the area.

For the next few days, the creatures checked out their new home surroundings and hunted for food in abundance.

Chapter 30 - Jackson Stone, Tour Guide

Campsites and hiking trails were leading from the small towns of Quilcene and Sequim westward and up into the wilderness toward the mountains and the creature's new cave entrance. This area was much like the Skokomish Wilderness area, and people liked to hike the trails.

Jackson Stone was the happy-go-lucky tour guide from the little town of Quilcene. He had been a tour guide for several years but sometimes got bored with it all. Being single, he lived alone in his quant tiny one-bedroom apartment. He was a naturalist and loved being out in nature, so during the summer months and on his time off work, he liked to hike up into the wilderness where there were a lot of thick woods. He would camp out in the remote forest for a few nights and pick up a few fish to each during the day to clear his head. He always brought his favorite weed; he liked to smoke, which he enjoyed in the open space.

He loved staring up at the stars at night, and it empowered him and made him feel free. He would take his small one-person tent and what little essentials he needed. Even though he was not a hunter, he would take along a handgun to scare off bears or other animals if they got too close. He loved to get away from the hectic everyday life of taking tourists around the area and talking about the same old things, and answering the same old questions on every tour.

It was near the end of June and perfect weather for him to take one of his much-needed excursions. He had a couple of days to kill, so he got up in the wake of dawn and headed for his favorite place to camp. Even though the trail was wide enough, it would be easy to get lost if you ventured from it. His favorite spot was about eight miles deep into the forest, and it took him a good three hours to get there but going to the place he loved made it feel like a short trip.

Once there, he found the clearing where he had set up his tent many times before and made camp. After he relaxed for a few hours and had lunch, he decided to take a wilderness walk a little deeper into the woods and enjoy being one with nature. He enjoyed his tranquility as he collected a few mushrooms when the clouds began to accumulate, and it became overcast and dark. By the time he got back to camp, it was just starting to get dusk, and he made a small campfire and had chili beans and a couple of hot dogs for dinner, simple and easy but filling.

Then he heard the strange chatter and whooping sounds of the creatures and then a deep echoing scream not too far off in the distance. It startled him because he had been in the forest for many years and never heard anything like that. Yes, the creatures had made it into the Buckhorn Wilderness and were now on their hunt for food once again, human food.

Before he heard the creature's scream, he was enjoying his solitude with his favorite weed, but it was rudely interrupted by the spine-chilling scream. Unnerved, he let the fire die down as he turned on his flashlight and looked around in the woods before he went to bed for the night. It unnerved him so much he decided to retire early.

He crawled into the small tent and then into his soon-to-be, a warm sleeping bag. While lying there and trying to go to sleep, he heard the scream of the creature not far away once again, and it was closer and in the tree line than before. It gave him the creeps as he felt the shivers shoot up his spine. He had never heard anything in the forest that uneased him as much as that scream. He gathered himself, grabbed his flashlight and pistol, crawled out of the tent, turned the light toward the tree line, and looked around. Not seeing anything, he heard some more whooping sounds like some animals communicating with each other. He thought, "What the heck can that be." He strained his brain to try to remember anything that sounded like what he was hearing. Whispering, "It's probably just a mother bear and her cubs," He didn't want to give into his fears because he was several miles from town, and it would've been a tough trip home in the dark. He thought that if he got back in his tent and pulled up his sleeping bag, it would give him the security he wanted and desperately needed.

Just as he made it back into his sleeping bag, he heard the heavy walking of the creature as it was getting close to his tent. Thinking it was a bear, he yelled, "Get out of here bear, get out of here," as loud as he could. He had pulled out his loaded pistol and had it right beside his sleeping bag. The footsteps continued right up to the front of his tent, and within an instant, the creature reached in with one arm and pulled out his sleeping bag with him still in it. It happened so quickly that he dropped his pistol on the ground next to where he had been lying. He started yelling and kicking, but it didn't deter the creature. It grabbed the top of the sleeping bag, right above his head, and threw it over his shoulder.

Realizing he couldn't get free from the creature's grip, he stopped kicking and screaming after several minutes and sat in a fetal position as he tried to figure out how he could escape. He knew it wasn't a bear because it was too big and too strong sounding, plus a bear would've just taken his food and left him alone. Now he began to realize a scary thought; he may be the creature's food.

He bounced around on the creatures back while being carried for a few miles deeper into the forest. When the creatures got to the cave entrance and its hiding place, Jackson heard that same strange-sounding chatter as the creature threw him hard to the ground. It knocked the breath out of him, so he rolled around inside his sleeping bag, trying to catch his breath, and then lay still, as if he were dead, just in case it was a bear that had carried him off. The creature, thinking he may have killed Jackson, became temporally distracted as he and the female went down into the cave to feast on their previous deer kill.

Jackson didn't waste any time as he rolled out of the sleeping bag and took off running down the trail as fast as he could run. He was scared out of his wits as he kept saying, "Don't kill me; please don't kill me." He just knew that at any moment, the creature was going to pounce on him from behind or maybe tackle him and kill him. He believed he was truly running for his life, and now the trip back seemed like it was taking him forever.

He couldn't believe it when he made it back to his tent without being captured again. He quickly reached inside and grabbed his pistol and then kept running toward town. By the time he made it about half-way down the trail toward town, he had heard the creatures coming up behind him. He stopped and turned around and quickly fired a few rounds toward the creatures as he yelled, "Take this, you Bastards." It instantly stopped them in their tracks, and they appeared to be afraid of the gunshots, so after a few minutes reluctantly gave up their pursuit of him.

A scared and shaken, Jackson made it back to town by the time it was almost dawn. He tried to find someone he could tell his story, too, but everyone was still asleep. Hoping the creatures hadn't followed him back to town, he decided to run to his apartment and take refuge inside. He grabbed his rifle and loaded it, and once he was able to calm himself down, he made himself a coffee and sat there, trembling and shaking from his experience. He relived the entire event as he thought back on how lucky he was to get away from the creatures alive. He whispered, "I'm never going back into those woods again."

As soon as it was daylight, he started looking for the county Sherriff to tell him what had happened to him.

Chapter 31 - The Inner Strength

Zak, Seth, and Julie went out on hunts several times in the past three weeks looking to kill the creatures but hadn't had any luck finding them. On their last search, Zak said, "Hey guys, listen! Do you notice anything different?"

Seth replied, "Yeah, I can hear the birds in the trees again, and there's wildlife out here in the forest."

"Exactly," exclaimed Zak. "I don't think the creatures are here anymore, they either moved somewhere else, or the Aliens came and got them." I'm not getting that eerie feeling of being watched all the time while we're out here, like before."

Julie said, "Do you really think they're gone?"

Zak said, "I sure hope so. I don't like hearing about people being killed in our woods."

Coming back into town from the walk through the woods and feeling more comfortable with the wilderness than they had for several weeks, Zak, Julie, and Seth were looking forward to having a pleasant drive in and grabbing some food at the Pizzeria in Lilliwaup.

"Combination or pepperoni and mushroom," Zak said as he steered his truck into the side street facing the restaurant.

"Let's do it up. The works," Julie laughed.

The car was a fast one. Powerfully built and strong lines, it was truly worthy of the Moniker, "muscle car." As it traveled through the western states, the new Ford Mustang GT, which had been purchased and picked up at the Ford motor company warehouse in Detroit, Michigan, growled smoothly and efficiently. Its new owner was feeling slightly euphoric in the excitement of the moment-to-moment momentum.

Hoping to reach Puget Sound in Washington State midday tomorrow, he hoped to board him and the Ford on the ferry to go to Vancouver Island. He wanted to Rendezvous with the film crew filming the new series, Northern Skies, which he had been chosen as a cast member from an exhaustive audition process.

Unfamiliar with these parts of the Pacific Northwest, he traveled partly by GPS and partly by memory of an earlier film he was on in a live shoot set in the state of Washington and had decided to take the shortcut through the mountains rather than the south-westerly highway 5.

The little town was one the muscle car driver had never been through but knew it would be perfect as a pit stop for food and fuel. Seeing a sign on a corner that read Bessie's Diner, he quickly revived the powerful V8 engine and sped forward, and at that exact moment, his left eye caught sight of a large flashing sign which read

Fresh Pizza. "That's it, that's what I want," and he pulled left sharply to enter the Pizzeria restaurant parking lot, not seeing the woman and her two children had entered the crosswalk at that exact time.

Zak had just pulled into the Pizzeria parking lot and turning off the engine. He turned to Julie and, at the moment, saw a big black car enter the parking lot also and run full onto a woman, narrowly missing the two children walking with her. The black vehicle immediately stopped, but Zak could see the person pinned under the car's front part.

Without thinking, Zak jumped out of his truck and ran to the car with the pinned victim. Zak grabbed the front bumper of the vehicle and immediately began to lift the front driver area. The strain was almost unbearable, and yet Zak felt a strange inner strength come to him, and a surge ran through him as he heard the woman s voice say "higher," higher." He lifted the vehicle higher to over a foot off the ground as Seth and another passerby pulled the woman safely from beneath the car. Seeing the woman seemingly out of danger and getting to her feet, Zak lowered the car down to the road.

He turned to look at Seth, standing staring at Zak as Seth said, shaking his head. "How did you do that, Zak? That car weighs over 3000 pounds!"

Zak looked at Seth and then looked down as he stared at the palms of his hands.

Chapter 32 - Unsuspecting Campers

It was pitch black in the forest and not a sound coming from the birds or wildlife at three in the morning. The creatures were angry with themselves; the male had a nasty scowl on his face as they left the comfort of their nest deep in the cave and went on their hunt. They had recklessly let the tasty meat of Jackson Stone get away from them, a mistake they would not make again.

The male walked ahead of the female with an act of defiance as they searched the woods. They were no longer looking for a mule deer but instead, the likes of a human. They headed east along the trail toward town until they came to what they were looking to find. In the middle of a small meadow sat two occupied tents and a fire smoldering from a small campfire. The light-colored smoke was gently rising into the sky as a young man and woman were asleep in one tent and a single male in the other.

The male made a gesture to the female to say, and it is what we are hunting. She looked back with a gesture of acceptance. They crept around the campsite, not making any sounds until the sun starting to show its face over the crest of the mountain. Then they patiently waited for the campers to emerge from their tents as they watched from a nearby tree line.

The first person to crawl out of his tent was the single male, and they watched as he went behind a tree and took a much-needed pee. When he finished, he looked around the campsite and then stretched his arms into the sky and took in the fresh morning air. Not seeing any guns with him, the creatures believed he could be easy prey and their next meal.

Jacob Tensely was a computer software designer for a firm in Seattle, and he wasn't much of a camper, preferring the good life of the city to be in the woods and roughing it. His older brother Richard and wife Sandra had talked him into going with them on this camping trip to get away from things for the weekend. Richard and Sandra each worked for a local newspaper company in Seattle.

It was only a few minutes later when Richard and Sandra each peeked their heads out of the tent, and Sandra said, "Man, it's cold out there. I have to put on my sweatshirt," as she retreated into the tent.

Richard, seeing that Jacob was up and about, crawled out of the warm, comfortable sleeping bag and said, "I'll make us some coffee."

Sandra didn't like the idea of going two and a half days without a shower, and she had already sampled the ice-cold water of the nearby small lake the day before. She told Richard she wasn't about to freeze her butt off in that water because it was like an ice cube.

The creatures were patient as they watched their prey from a distance in the tree line. They could have killed them at any time they wanted but chose to wait until the darkness of night came again. There was no moon out, and it was pitch black in the forest once again, and they wanted to use the cover of darkness. It would make it easier to sneak up a little closer to their prey before they attacked.

For the entire day, the creatures observed every move the three made. They followed along the trail from a distance as the three took a couple of fishing poles, and the guys caught several small fish in the nearby lake. Sandra picked berries while the guys fished. They cleaned the fish and then went back to camp to have lunch.

The creatures were chattering with each other, using whooping and grunting sounds, and Sandra said, "Hey guys, what kind of sound is that?"

Richard replied, "I have no idea." They laughed it off as Jacob made light of it by acting like a monkey. They were oblivious to the danger that lies in wait for them.

Later that day, they stoked the fire and got it going again as they listened to music and cooked up the fish for dinner. They enjoyed their quiet time in the forest until after dark when they all decided to go to bed. That is when all hell broke loose.

The creatures had inched their way along and snuck up where they were within only a few yards of the tents. They hid in the bushes until the right moment to strike. When he was ready, the male looked over at the female and gave her a slight nod, and then the two of them attacked their victims with lightning speed. The male pounced on Richard and the female on Sandra, and she barely had time to let out a death-defying scream. It happened so fast their last thought must have been that bears had attacked them. Within an instant, the two bodies lie mangled and dead on the ground, and the creatures were standing over them with blood dripping from their long fangs.

Jacob was standing there in shock for a few seconds when he realized what just happened. Seeing the angry scowl in the creature's eyes and face sent panic through his body, and he took off running toward town. The creatures were not concerned about him, and they now had the fresh meat of two humans they wanted. The male took Richard's body and threw it over his shoulder, and the female threw Sandra's body over her shoulder. Then they headed deeper into the forest for the safety of their cave hideout.

Jacob was able to make it to town by the early morning hours, battered and beaten from the bushes and limbs sticking out along the trail, along with the battered part of this brain from losing his brother and sister-in-law. He found the Sheriff Department and pushed open the door as he screamed out. "They killed Richard and Sandra!" For that brief second, he thought, "I can still hear Sandra's last agonizing scream. It was horrible."

The people in the Sheriff's office immediately went to his aid and asked him what he was saying. He was breathing heavily as he sat down and said, "Some bears or some other kind of creatures killed them while we were camping up there in the woods." The girls in the office immediately contacted the Deputy and told him what had happened. It didn't take long, and the Deputy was at the office, and he began asking Jacob exactly what had taken place. Jacob told him where they were camped out along the trail about seven or eight miles up in the forest when two bears or something attacked them.

The Deputy tried to get Jacob to take him to where the killings happened, and he said, "I know that my brother and sister-in-law are dead. Those damn creatures killed them. I'm not ever going back into the woods again, and if I were you, Deputy, I would take an entire team of well-armed men with me when you go up there. Those creatures are killers, and they'll kill you too."

Chapter 33 - The Oreos

Blaine had one job. Only the one. Don't fuck up. Leaving from Bend, Oregon, to the Olympic National Park, his job was to be the designated driver. When the rest of the gang were slightly inebriated or madly plastered, he was the non-drinking driver and, "Don't fuck up, guy."

Blaine, Mark, Todd, and Brad, being university students in Bend, knew their road trip was not only going to be the best but sorely needed. "We're going to hit every microbrewery from here to Seattle," Mark exclaimed as he threw a well-padded duffel bag in the van. "Man, I am super excited," he shouted.

Brad only yawned loudly and nodded, "Yup, yup," as long as I can sleep the first leg."

Todd came running up with a case of American lager beer and threw it in the van also. "You sure I can't convince you to convert Blaine," Todd ribbed, "One beer won't hurt."

"Mark replied, forget it, man, he's a non-drinker, and our ride, don't fuck him up," and they all laughed.

Blaine knew the route well; his aunt and uncle had lived in Olympia, Washington, and his family traveled from his home in Portland, Oregon, many times over the years. But this was the first trip he would be taking as an adult, and with these crazy lug-heads. Friends through the last three years at college had made them close and highly respectful of each other, which is why Blaine volunteered to be the designated driver on the trip. Rarely drinking alcohol, he didn't mind the drive and wouldn't mind the camaraderie, as long as he could stand the beer belching and bad jokes.

Deciding to stop in Olympia, Blaine suggested they stay at the cheap Dew Drop Inn situated on the north end of town for the night. "Great idea," Todd said, in between yawns. "Those last two breweries were for shit, and I'm bushed."

They all nodded in agreement.

As Blaine parked the van and started to exit, Mark, who had held back, said, "Come here, man," As he grabbed his duffel and began to rummage through it. Blaine walked over and said, "What's up," putting his hands in his jacket pockets, a slight chill had moved in.

"Hey, dude, just for protection, I want you to see this and know I have it." Mark pulled half-way from his bag, a small barrel Smith and Wesson five-chamber 357 revolver. "It's all legal, I'm certified, and it's registered, but any shit happens, it's here, Cool!"

"Damn!" "Yeah, it's cool, man! Just don't think we'll need it." Blaine replied, "You brought a friggin gun?" Blaine smiling said, as he lightly pushed Mark while they walked toward the hotel. Mark just grinned.

The next day they left the Inn around noon to their next destination. Pulling into the park, Blaine gunned Van's engine, hoping to make their campsite before dark. "How much longer?" Brad belched, "We've got about another hour to the high country and then maybe another forty-five minutes to the site. Just chill, and hey, hand me those Oreos."

When they got to the campsite, it was dark, and all four were tired, and the three more than a little drunk. Todd and Brad were sleeping and clearly couldn't be moved. Blaine suggested, "Let those guys sleep. I'm going to stay up a bit," worked up from the drive. Mark ambled over and said, "I'll hang with you," and started to build a small fire with wood left from a previous burn in the burn pit at their site.

Blaine moved toward the wood's mere feet away from their site to relieve himself and walked in about 10 feet. Turning the flashlight off, he stood with the light in his left hand and an Oreo cookie half-way in his mouth. Standing there feeling the cool air and vibrant sounds of the forest, he felt refreshed after the long drive and could feel his neck muscles begin to relax.

A scurry ran in front of him, and he instantly turned on the light. They're sitting on his haunches was a good-sized raccoon. "Hey, little fella," Blaine said. "Sure, cute," And tossed him the Oreo from his mouth. The little beggar waddled over and took the cookie in his hands, and began to eat it. "Cool," Blaine said and turned around, and briskly walked back to the site.

Mark looked up from his cell phone as Blaine approached and reached for several Oreos. "I'll be right back, man," Blaine said as he turned and trotted back to the forest edge. Mark, who was standing, grunted and pulled his arms back and stretched. Blaine turned the flashlight on once again as he knelt, but now in the light, there were dozens of little begging raccoons with outstretched hands requesting their share. Blaine set the flashlight down momentarily to reach into his jacket pocket to retrieve more cookies, inadvertently turning off the light and hearing the rapid scurrying of the critters.

Bringing the flashlight up, he turned it on in the direction of the raccoons. But none were there, and, in their place, stood a monster. The darkness shadowed the creature but highlighted the immense size. Blane instantly felt the back of his neck run cold, and his throat caught in mid-scream, and he fell backward. The creature moved forward, and the face which so resembled a human opened its mouth, and the protrusion of teeth and jutting incisors hung open. Oddly enough, Blaine could see the creature was female, with its undulating breast moving as it walked.

Suddenly from behind Blaine, twenty feet away, a shot rang out toward the sky, and the creature, in one swift movement, cleared ten feet back into the woods and was gone. Mark ran up to Blaine and hysterically yelled, mother fucker. MOTHER FUCKER." as the 357 hung by the ready. Helping Blaine to his feet, he excitedly said, "Dude, that was the biggest grizzly I've ever seen."

Blaine, in a state of semi shock, ran back to the van with Mark matching his steps. They both jumped in the van, and Mark yelled, "Let's get the fuck out of here," And Blaine sped out through the campground toward the road. All Blaine could keep saying as they reached the road was, "That was not a bear. That was not a bear."

Chapter 34 - The Bad Decision

Jake Sweeney and Farley Oates were out of their element. "You know what town this is?" Farley asked as Jake drove the later model Cadillac into Quilcene's bustling little town nestled in the Buckhorn Wilderness area's eastern edge.

"No clue," Jake responded. "But it should work to rest up for a night," as he pulled over to the Shell service station. "I'll fill us up. Can you grab me a pack of Lucky's? Non-filters if they have em."

Farley eyed left to right nervously, looking to keep a low profile, and then looked down as he walked over to the station's store. Having earlier robbed the Spokane Washington National Bank, they were none too eager to draw attention to themselves.

Jake scanned the small village as he pumped the gas and noticed it to be a busy and lively place full of tourists. "That'll do well," He murmured. In the morning, they would make a faster clip and get to the Canadian border after picking up their new passports and ware in Mount Vernon.

British Columbia would be an excellent place to lay up a few days before making the northern loop back to Chicago. This job had been planned carefully with the assistance of a young bank teller Jake had shacked up with off and on before she moved to Spokane, "To escape the "dreariness" of Chicago, as she put it. Spokane offered her an opportunity to work in a job that offered good pay and wide-open spaces.

But Sharon was a criminal at heart and cunning, not opposed to the infrequent use of recreational drugs that included Cocaine. It eventually prompted her to contact Jake and tell him about the fabulous setup she had and the easy chance to procure more than two million dollars on a particular drop, at a specific time, at her specific bank. Jake readily consented and grabbed Farley, his associate in crime, to be his number two. Farley was more than eager and ready.

The bank was not busy that day, but the armored car parked out front had issued a request that all new traffic be halted that was going into the bank. Jake and Farley, already inside the bank, took this opportunity to storm the armored car drivers and grab the bags that held just a tad over one million dollars.

"Everyone lay the hell down," Jake yelled and then looked at Sharon and pulled the trigger of his 1911 Colt 45 automatic and blowing the back of her head out, spraying blood, brain matter, and viscera in the direction of the next teller. "Unless you want what that bitch got, you'll stay down," he yelled. Then he and Farley ran out the front door firing their pistols at the guard posted in the cab of the armored car. Jumping into the Chevy Caprice and speeding toward their waiting for another hidden vehicle, a 1990 Cadillac Deville. "Good shot."

Farley said. Jake looked over at Farley and said, "Dead women tell no lies," and smirked.

The old trooper scanned the incoming traffic and gathering crowds and felt good that everything was running smoothly and in order. Aside from the minor traffic hiccup and teenage ruckus, all was going well except the older Cadillac that had pulled into the shell station.

Tom had been in law enforcement and a state trooper for 38 years and has worked as a Washington state trooper for 13 of those years, and he knew the state well, particularly the highway system. He'd been called in to assist with the abundance of tourists that would be pouring into Quilcene, raising the town's population from a general 600 to over 20,000 in the course of a three-day Redbud Film and Food Festival.

His memory was keen, having been alerted to two men of the same age and builds, aside from the facial hair the perps sported during the Spokane robbery; these two fit their description sent out over the state-wide law enforcement network. Tom's passion aside from his family and career was his love of the legendary Texas Rangers and how their pursuit of the criminal kind was epic. He related to the intricate workings of the Ranger's processes and pursuit tactics, and these two pinged his radar.

Waiting until they had entered their vehicle again, he followed them to a quiet and less used area of town. Finding no warrants or outstanding need to pull them over, he continued his pursuit. Jake saw the trooper's vehicle staying back in pursuit. He had been in the criminal game long enough to understand the law officer's mind as well and knew they were spotted. The officer decided to pull them over to clear this up and get back to his festival duties.

As Tom walked up to the Cadillac, Farley, in a move of excited agitation, pulled his Berretta 9mm pistol and shot Tom twice in the chest area as the trooper bent down to their car window. Tom fell back and was stunned as he patted his chest in pain and pulled his uniform blouse apart to look at his Kevlar vest with the two Barretta's bullets embedded in it, as the Cadillac peeled out in a rush of gravel and dust. Winching, he reached for his radio and barked into it the vital information of Jake and Farley's vehicle. Then leaning back, he said, "Officer down, but getting up," and cursed.

Jake speeding out of town, which now became a tiny spot in his rear-view mirror, looked at Farley and said, "Damn Farley, that was a bad decision."

Farley only continued to look down as he quickly reloaded his pistol. "You know where you're headed?" Farley said, looking up as he continued to work his gun.

"To the high country," Jake responded. I figure if we shoot up into the forest, we can pick another car from campers or anglers.

"Now that's a bad decision. I don't know anything about the woods, do you?" Farley asked angrily.

Jake just stared straight ahead and pushed the engine to the higher elevation. The evening light was starting to fade, and Farley said: "Stop, back up. I thought I saw a road back there to campsites." "If we can come onto a car, I can get it started, and we can use it and ditch this one." If there was one thing Farley could do well, it was hot wire and steal cars, something he had been doing in Chicago all his life. Night had set, and Jake parked the Cadillac in the thick forest and stood beside it as he pulled on a Lucky taken from its pack. "Stick here, and I'll grab one of those cars from the grounds down there."

Jake just nodded as he took another pull on his luck, knowing that Farley was more than qualified for the task.

The forest was now fully immersed in the night, and light strained to peer through the trees. Farley was adept at nighttime ventures and though not used to maneuvering over the thick underbrush, felt he was not so much out of his element when it came to theft.

Spurred on by the excitement of the deed, he leaned against a thick tree on the outer edge of the campsite where the vehicles were parked. He took a step to go forward, and he felt a hand lay on the back of his neck. It was a big hand, and the fingers covered around his neck. As he struggled to turn around to see his assailant, the grip became tighter and held him fast forward. Farley, frightened and agitated, once again tried to turn his head and yell out but could only manage a squeak.

The male creature slowly turned his wrist, which turned Farley's head to face the creature, and Farley let out a muffled scream. "It's a Bigfoot, and the creature opened its mouth wide and bit down hard on Farley's face, which separated from his body to hang in the mouth of the monster as it began to chew, then reached down and pulled Farley's twitching body by his right arm, through the thick forest.

Jake, slowly growing agitated and impatient with Farley's extended return, threw his cigarette down, and started to crawl into the Cadillac. Suddenly and without warning, he was hit with a force that threw him several feet in front of the car. Striving to stay alert, while losing consciousness, a second force lifted him. With a hideous rake of her claw-like fingernails, the female creature eviscerated Jake and threw his body against a tall stand of boulders, killing him instantly. The female pulled her arms together in a show of strength and let out a deep and long scream that pierced the night.

The million dollars sat in a durable suitcase untouched in the trunk as the female creature vented her rage on the now being mangled Cadillac.

Chapter 35 - Driven back to Skokomish Wilderness

One of the deputies where Richard and Sandra were killed was in touch with Sheriff Kane, and he told Kane the Bears that had been doing the killings in Kane's area had moved north and had killed a couple of campers up in the mountain area not far from town.

Kane said, "I got something to tell you, Franklin, those creatures aren't bears. I got an up-close and personal look at them myself."

Franklin asked, "Then what the hell are they, Sheriff?"

Kane replied, "I don't know for sure, but I know they sure and the hell aren't bears, and they're not human either, so I don't know what the hell they are."

Franklin said, "Well, I'm putting together a search party tomorrow with a group of armed hunters to go up in the woods and see if we can find them. If we do, we will kill them for you, Philip. Also, Phil, we had the craziest thing happen. Remember last week on those reports telling about that big robbery from that Spokane bank?"

"Yes,"

Franklin said, "Well, we recovered a little over one million dollars in the trunk of a torn-up Cadillac in the forest above Quilcene. A trooper up here identified it as the car with the perps that did the job, the sons of bitches shot him, thank god for Kevlar, he's fine, but we believe the million dollars is the bank money, but no bodies have been found, as yet."

The indigenous Bigfoot or Sasquatch is a non-human entity that has lived in the Pacific Northwest for as long as human inhabitants have lived in and settled the region's lower areas. Very well-known and revered by the various Indian communities in the state, the Sasquatch is looked at as a people who inhabit the forest. They are adapted to living in that environment just as humans are adapted to theirs.

Officially, the being does not exist, but unofficially, Washington state is one of the only states in the United States that protect and have a law against the hunt or killing of the being. Even posting signs in the forest to be aware and do not disrupt or harm the being. As such, a pleasant peace has existed between man and their kind.

Once the killer creatures showed up in the forest, several family groups of indigenous Bigfoots living in the area for years moved deeper into the mountain area and stayed away from the killers. They didn't like what the creatures were doing to the humans, and they'd never killed a human and ate it as these two creatures had done. They were angry about it. They kept to themselves and hidden away in the remote wilderness areas, not wanting any confrontations with humans.

The next day the search party made it into the forest at daybreak, armed and ready to kill what they believed was some bear/bigfoot creature. The Deputy told everyone not to shoot the Bigfoot creatures unless it appeared to be a threat to them. One of the hunters said under his breath to another hunter, "I'm not going to wait until one of us gets killed before I shoot that thing."

The other hunter whispered, "Yeah, me either, I'm out here to kill these things, so they don't kill one of us or someone else from town. It is going to ruin our tourist trade if we don't stop them soon."

They trekked through the forest for most of the morning, but the two killer creatures took refuge deep in the cave. The hunters had spread out and covered a lot of ground until they got to the steep areas of the mountains. That is when the hunters spotted one of the indigenous Bigfoot, and it was moving higher into the upper cave area.

It was over two hundred yards away, and the forest was becoming steeper and more challenging to climb, so the hunter that said he was going to kill the creature took aim and pulled the trigger of his weapon. A loud shot rang out and ended the silence the hunters had been experiencing the last few miles. Right behind his shot was another one from the other hunter that had said he was going to kill the Bigfoot as soon as they spotted one as well. Thankfully, both bullets missed their mark as the Bigfoot ducked away to safety.

Franklin caught up with the two hunters and said, "What the hell are you guys doing? Do you even know if the Bigfoot you shot at is the same creature we've been hunting?"

One of the hunters said, "You do what you got to do, Deputy, but as far as I'm concerned, right now, there's no such thing as a good bigfoot to me. I'm going to shoot any of them, I see."

Franklin said, "Ok, that's it; this hunt is over." He immediately called everyone together and called off the search. He said, "We're done here; just be careful on the way back and try not to shoot each other along the way." He was angry with the two hunters, but he understood their frustration.

The next day a group of the male indigenous Bigfoots got together with their clan and talked about what had happened with the hunters. They didn't like that the humans were now shooting at them, and it was all because of what the creatures had done to the campers. They knew they had to do something to drive the creatures away from their home there in Buckhorn Wilderness. They knew if they didn't, the humans wouldn't give up until they killed a couple of them and said they were the killer creatures that had been terrorizing everyone in the forest.

After their meeting, they split up in their quest to find the two creatures and hoping the humans didn't come back in the process and kill one or several of them with their high-powered rifles. They each had huge tree limbs as they searched the forest for them. They decided that if the creatures didn't leave their area, they would all come together once they found them and bludgeon them to death.

Keeping a vigilant eye out for humans, they searched the forest until they spotted the creatures not too far from the cave entrance and their hiding place. They looked as though they were heading out for another hunt when the indigenous Bigfoots started giving whoops, grunts and screams, and they began closing in on the creatures. Realizing something was wrong, the creatures began giving their cries back to the Bigfoots. The creatures didn't like what they heard from the Bigfoots as the local Bigfoot group conveyed to them that they were no longer welcome in that part of the forest. The group leader told them that they had to go back to where they had come from, or the group would kill them. At first, the big male grew angry and braced himself for a fight as he let out a slight yell. Then he saw that several of the large male Bigfoots were coming after them with clubs. He believed they might've been able to fight off a few of them, but not seven or eight of them at the same time. The two were ferocious killers but no match for the odds that were now stacked against them.

Not willing to risk the life of himself or his female companion, they decided to head down into the cave and away from the dangers of the advancing Bigfoots. The local Bigfoots followed them into the cave and chased after them for several miles underground before giving up the chase. They threatened them with their clubs and told them not to return to their area.

The creatures decided to go back to the Skokomish Wilderness; it was more like a home to them anyway. They had great luck hunting for wildlife, and the humans were easy prey in that area. They knew they would have to be a little more cunning and resourceful to try and avoid the local people's guns. Maybe, even expand their hunting area to the outer limits of the Skokomish Wilderness.

Chapter 36 - The Return

One of the fascinating things about aliens that have always been speculated is whether they have a form of infrared vision naturally in their optic nerve or is a result of technology built into the spacesuit the aliens wear. As it turns out, their natural genetic makeup includes scotopic vision, and the hybrid creatures, having been given the gene of the aliens and the nocturnal sense of the bear DNA, inherited this feature. It enabled them to traverse the myriad of passageways, canals, and formations that made up the cave system.

The journey back was not an easy one nor a short one and took them five days to make. The many forms of cave dwellings subterranean animals provided minimal sustenance, but the creature's appetite was voracious, and bigger and more plentiful food would need to be found.

On the fifth day, the creatures emerged from the cave system and had one all-powerful mission, FIND FOOD. Night had already descended on the Skokomish wilderness when they arrived, and this gave them an immense sense of comfort as they were proficient at night hunting.

Many animals hunt at night in the forest, and for many reasons, the cover of darkness provides stealth. It is where the creatures excelled. The Sasquatch DNA gave them the ability to navigate the uneven and thick underbrush of the forest with a ninja's nimbleness. Coupled with the alien being's intelligence and the ferociousness of the grizzly, they were an unequaled Predator.

All of that came into play when they came upon their food source. The Five Timberwolves were well into the second hour in eating from the Large Elk they had brought down earlier in the evening. It had been a glorious battle. The Elk bleating as he finally succumbed to the many tears and rips to its limbs and the killing bite to the hapless animal's neck inflicted by the huge packs' leader.

The creatures made their way close to the kill, then making themselves known, though surely the wolves would flee, leaving their prize unprotected. But that was not the case. This pack, all mature, weathered, and battle-proven warriors, stood their ground, and lifted their heads, and exposed their huge canine fangs.

The leader, weighing over 200 pounds, sauntered toward the creatures and slowly growled, exposing his teeth. The male and female creatures both emerged into the moonlight and, standing side by side, did the same, exposing their fangs as well. The leader's Lieutenant joined his side and readied himself for any advance these interlopers would make toward their kill.

In a fit of frenzied hunger, the male creature ran right through the two sentries and grabbed a hunk of the elk's flesh. The wolves immediately swarmed the male and began their tearing at him. The female, feeling her fury along with her extreme hunger, grow to an apex ran at her mate to join the fray.

As three of the wolves lay dead and a fourth having ran free, the large leader limped away, leaving the slaughter. The male and female creatures looked around, saw no further threat, dropped to their knees, and began to feast.

Chapter 37 - Call of the Wild

Unknown to the creatures was a small tracking device placed in each calves' calves, which perfectly melded with their flesh. It had been transmitting to the alien craft since its debarking of the hybrid creation.

The aliens observed the movements of the creatures. Stepping up to the next stage of the experiment, the aliens transmitted a command to the receiver device (much like a cell phone would transmit a command to a device on Earth, only much more powerful and far-reaching). The receiving device emitted a group of minuscule nanobots into the creature's bloodstream, which separated and spread throughout the body.

The robotic pods, each containing a highly concentrated dose of Earth's influenza, burst open and disbursed its lethal content. The results should show within twenty-four Earth hours whether the creation was susceptible to the Earth virus or not.

On the third day after their return, the creatures had not fed since their feast on the Elk. Once again felt their hunger rise to a fervor and set out to obtain food. The creatures walked through the forest, remembering areas from previous travel before heading to the northern wilderness. The male looked at the female and chattered a few words of their language, but little was needed due to their slight telepathic connection. Yes, the lower woods cabin would be good to travel to and, possibly food or shelter would be there. The cabin was a quaint older cabin situated by a small lake at the center of the wilderness. Over the years, the owners had used it as a fishing retreat, who now only used it once or twice a year.

The creatures approached the clearing edges where the cabin sat and, eyeing the area, making sure no one was present, made their way to the doorway. The door's lock was an old one and took little resistance from the male's weight to burst it open. As they walked into the cabin, the female immediately began rummaging through the interior's contents. Seeing no foodstuffs or anything of use, the large male became enraged and proceeded to demolish the entire inner space, flinging cabinets to the far side of the other room; the refrigerator overturned and mangled.

Then both creatures stopped and as together lifted their faces to the ceiling as a high-pitched squeal rang out, just outside the cabin. The wild boar or feral hog is a misunderstood animal. Unless you are a hunter, most people don't take much notice of this beast while they are in the woods until they are right on you.

The older male boar weighed more than 300 pounds, and his razor-sharp tusks were large for his size. The boar had approached the cabin thinking humans had come back, having seen them arrive in the past, and he was hungry. He had not opposed killing a human and eating them before and was not afraid, cautious, but not afraid.

As he approached the cabin, he squealed loudly to alert his tribe. More intelligent than a dog, the pig's mind was already formulating his plan of attack, but he would need his group. The creatures knew the sound well, and, sensing food, they made their way to the back of the cabin to slip into the forest and then flank the waiting meal.

The creatures sprang onto the boar, who stood facing the front door, waiting for his group. Taken by surprise and not expecting an assailant of their size, the boar stiffened in fear. Now he was afraid. As the creatures tore into the big male pig, the other pigs could only watch from a safe distance. Once again feeling his superiority, the male creature let out a long low trumpeting roar followed by several more.

Dan and Patricia Bowers were at their campground, which bordered the lake and cabin. Enjoying the comfort inside their RV, Dan turned on his cell phone video camera and started to film his wife making their bed happily. "Having fun, honey pie?" Dan said. Suddenly, a low screaming roar was heard in the distance, and Dan captured it on his phone.

"What is that?" Patricia said as they stood there, listening to it.

"I've never heard that sound before, "Dan said as they continued to listen. "Well, one thing for sure, that's the call of the wild, you never know what you're going to hear up here," he said, as they both stood and listened.

It had been well over 24 hours since the creatures received the Earth Virus. Showing no signs of susceptibility to the pathogen, this portion of the alien experiment had been a success.

Chapter 38 – Becky Takes a Wrong Turn

"Yes, Deputy," Becky's mom, Diane, frantically yelled out over the phone, she is missing. I got a call from her around midnight, and she said she had taken a wrong turn and was walking down the dirt road toward the main road. I think she was on Old Creek Road by the way it sounded."

Deputy Kenny Jones thought, "Oh no. That's where Sheriff Kane said he'd come face to face with the two killer creatures."

"Becky said she'd run out of gas and had been walking for a few hours because she couldn't reach anyone on her cell phone until she got a little lower down the mountain road. She said she wished she had just stayed in the car, but it was too late to turn back. She's been going to school at Washington State and hasn't been home since I moved here three years ago. We live the next dirt road further down, and she just got confused and took the wrong turn. I don't have a car right now, or I would find her. Her phone went dead while we were talking to each other." She talked to her mom and used her iPhone as a flashlight until it ran out of battery. "Can you please go check on her Deputy and see if you can find her? It's so dark out there; she's probably scared to death by now."

"Yes, I'll head up that way right now, Mrs. Collins," replied Deputy Jones. He immediately jumped in his patrol car and turned on the lights as he headed in that direction. On the way there, he was wondering if the creatures had come back, and maybe they had already gotten Becky.

Once it got dark in the forest, it was pitch black, and Becky could hardly see where she was walking. She was stumbling over rocks and small potholes as she fought desperately to keep her footing and find her way down the dusty road. She had experienced the fear of the forest once before when she was young. She had gotten lost in the woods for several hours during the night never forgot how frightened she was. Now she was feeling that same way once again. As she stumbled along, she thought, "When there's no moon in these damn woods, it's hard to imagine anything could be this dark. It's almost like being blind."

She needed to relieve her bladder, but she was too afraid to stop until the pain became almost unbearable. When she pulled her Jeans down and started to go, she heard the scream of the male creature, and it wasn't too far from her, just inside the tree line. It scared her so badly she immediately pulled up her pants while still going and wet her pants.

Her eyes widened to see the creature, but it was too dark to see more than a few yards in any direction. She immediately took off, running down the road as the two creatures slowly followed, being a little cautious that she didn't have a gun with her. Just a little further down the road, she reached a steep ravine near the edge of the road, tripped, and tumbled over the side. She rolled down about twenty feet and started crawling around, searching for a place to hide. She found an animal hole that was just wide enough for her to slide her body into the hole. She pushed herself into the hole, feet first, to about ten feet. By then, the creatures had moved in close to where she was hiding. Becky was crying and screaming at the top of her lungs as the creatures tried to grab her with their long arms and claws. She was in too deep for them to reach her. The female attempted to push her body into the hole, but she was too broad and thick. She screamed out in frustration for not being able to get her prey.

Deputy Jones had just made it onto the dirt road, turned off his flashing lights, and headed upward when he spotted the female creature going across the road in front of him. He stopped his vehicle, left it running, and jumped out with his 45 revolver in one hand and his flashlight in the other. He was trying to get a shot at her, thinking the creatures must have already killed Becky, and they were heading back up into the woods. As he walked slowly toward the creature, he couldn't get his pistol sites on her as she quickly moved toward the tree line. Then he heard the muffled screams of Becky coming from down the embankment. He had his pistol in both hands and out in front of him. He looked over the edge of the embankment. Not seeing any dangers, he didn't waste any time as he quickly went down to where Becky was hiding.

He had shined his light in on her and started to say he was Deputy Jones when the male creature hit him full force, knocking the gun and flashlight from his hand. It happened so fast he didn't even have time to defend himself. The creature sunk his long fangs into his neck and ripped at the flesh, almost decapitating him. He then dropped the Deputy's body to the ground and let out a thunderous scream, getting a response from the female across the road and in the woods. He picked up the deputy's body and threw him over his shoulder, no longer concerned with Becky.

Becky stayed hidden and terrified until daylight and then slowly crawled out of the hole, trembling and shaking. She grabbed the deputy's gun, lying on the ground, and ran to his pickup. It was still sitting in the middle of the road and running.

Chapter 39 - The Secret Weapon

The bar was lively, and the vibe was happening, but Zak and Seth were focused on other matters. Into the second pitcher of beer, they felt their passions grow more intense. "You know, we may not be done with those creatures. They could come back. Just like Shief did," Zak remarked. "That's it, man, if those bastards come back, let's end this."

Those fucking aliens, they're the ones that caused all this shit." Seth said, taking another drink of his beer.

"Yeah, well, with all the other shit that's happening in the world today," Zak said.

The pub's door opened, and Sheriff Kane walked through and spotted the two friends walked over and sat right down. "I know it's after hours, but is this an official visit or a beer run," Zak joked.

Kane bent his head sideways and laughed, "No tickets tonight."

"What's up to Sheriff, beer?" Seth asked as he reached for a clean mug from an extra on the table.

Kane nodded and said, "Guys, I'm sure we've got those damn creatures back, I've got a dead deputy, and Becky Collins ran out of gas up there on Old Creek Road. She said two large creatures came after her, and deputy Jones was killed and taken by the two creatures. She didn't know what kind of creatures they were, but they were huge and scary. I'm fed up and want to take care of this right away."

"What do you have in mind?" Zak asked.

"Glad you asked," Kane said, reaching for his beer. Let's step outside; I have something to show you.

Walking toward the sheriff's vehicle, Seth said, "Shit, I feel like I'm being arrested."

Kane said, "look at this," and lifted the back hatch of the cruiser to expose a good-sized box in hard grade metal box. Kane unlatched the hinges, and there sat a US M2A1 flame thrower. "Ever see one of these?" Kane asked.

"Many times, Zak said, as he stared at the object. "You know how to use it?"

Kane replied, "I got it from lockup evidence in Seattle; they gave it to me on loan, instructions, and all. Conventional methods haven't been working on those fuckers' lads. It is my secret weapon. I want to go out with three of my best men and end this once and for all, so are you two with me?

Zak and Seth both said, "Yes."

Chapter 40 - Creatures at Vera's House

It was just getting dusk when Zak's sister, Vera, had to go out and give the two calves and the mother some hay and grain and make sure they had enough water for the night. William usually did the feeding and watering, but he was out of town on business, so it was now Vera's chore. She didn't mind because it gave her and Kari a chance to spend some time together and enjoy the animals. As she left the house's safety and opened a few gates to the calf pen, Kari was right by her side. She excitedly jumped up and down from one leg to the other, mimicking the hungry and thirsty calves.

Vera was always vigilant once outside the house because of wolves, mountain lions, and bears. She was even more so now that Zak had told her about the creatures. They hadn't had any problems with any animals in the past few years, so she wasn't suspecting any danger. Once she fed the calves, she inadvertently looked toward the tree line as a matter of habit. For a moment, she thought she caught the faint outline image of a large animal as it moved from one tree to another. She froze and paralyzed in place as she squinted her eyes to make sure she didn't just imagine the shadows. Nothing, everything seemed calm and normal, so after a few minutes, she went about her chores. Then she caught a glimpse of the male creature out of the corner of her eye and turned to see. She got a full look at the monster, and it was a little closer and nearer the edge of the woods as it moved from tree to tree.

She instantly dropped the grain bucket and grabbed Kari by the hand. "What's the matter, mommy?" Kari yelled out.

Not wasting much time, Vera quickly headed for the house. She was almost dragging Kari as she said, "I saw something in the woods, and it looks like it's coming toward the house. We need to get inside and lock all the doors and windows." She didn't want to tell Kari what she thought she saw, afraid it would scare her even more.

Just as they made it inside the house, the large male let out a bellowing scream, and a frightened Kari screamed out in fear as she yelled, "What was that, mommy?" Not taking time to explain, Vera immediately got on the phone and called Zak. He was relaxing on his sofa as he said, "Hello."

A frightened and shaken Vera said, "Zak. Zak. Thank God for your home. William is out of town, and it's just Kari and me here alone. You gotta come quick. The creatures are here. I saw one of them, and it was moving toward the house. It just made a hellish scream just outside the tree line. Get here as soon as you can, Please."

Zak said, "Oh, Damn! Get your rifle out, and I'll be there as soon as I can."

He grabbed his Army night goggles and rifle and flew out the door. On the way there, he was hoping it wasn't going to be too late because it was going to take him ten minutes, driving as fast as he could go, to get there.

Vera grabbed the rifle and loaded it, and then turned all the lights off inside the house. She flipped the outside lights on. She could see out, but she believed the creatures couldn't see in, as she had Kari crawl under the dining table. She went over to the window, holding the rifle in her hands, and looked outside but couldn't see anything. She listened for any sound, but it had suddenly gotten eerily quiet and creepy. Then she heard the chattering sound coming from the creatures and knew they were moving from the woods toward the dark corners of the outside of the house.

When she looked outside again, she got a glimpse of one of the creatures, and it resembled a person, just like Zak had told her about the creatures. She could tell it was large, dark, and fast as it moved from one spot to another. They were carefully moving in on their prey when the male let out another bellowing scream. Kari screamed out again and put her hands over her ears.

After several minutes of silent terror, they heard the dreaded heavy footsteps of one of the creatures on the front porch. It moved from one side of the porch to the other and peered through the windows. Vera had her rifle in hand as she ran and crawled under the table with Kari. They were both trembling in fear and clinging to each other as they held each other in their arms.

The male creature had just knocked the front door down when Zak pulled into the driveway. Vera got a complete look at it with its long brown hair and thick muscular body. It looked around and then focused on them hiding under the table as it growled aloud and showed its teeth. She pointed the gun at it and was just about to pull the trigger when a shot rang out from outside.

Zak had quickly pulled up in front of the house, jumped out of his car, and leveled his rifle at the male. He got there just before the creatures started to move in on their next meal. When the bullet hit its target, the big male fell sideways and off the porch, but the bullet just grazed him right above his temple. It bounced off his skull and didn't penetrate his brain. Stunned and confused for a few seconds, he looked around and then stumbled back to his feet. He then quickly headed into the woods with the female right behind him. Zak took a couple more shots, but they were already deep in the thick forest, and it was hard to get an accurate shot at them because of the darkness. Once hidden in the forest and seeing that her mate was injured, the female turned around toward Zak and made a deep, bellowing scream of defiance.

Zak quickly went inside to see if Vera and Kari were okay. After seeing they were, he told them to wait for him, that he would go into the woods and see if he could find the creatures and kill them. Vera pleaded with him not to go, but he was angry and wanted to get the wounded monster.

He put on his night-vision goggles and headed in the direction he'd last seen the creatures enter the woods. He went into the thick forest about a quarter of a mile, and then the anger died down, and reasoning took over. He realized he was now on their turf and fighting their war. Feeling a little fear come over him, he figured he better get back to Vera and Kari before the creatures circled behind him and killed him or went back and grabbed the two girls.

When he got back to the house, he talked Vera and Kari into grabbing a few things where they could come and stay at his home until they could do something about the creatures. He told her he would come back tomorrow and put something over the front doorway and feed the animals. On the way back, Kari was sitting in the middle of the front seat and looked up at Zak and said, "I knew you'd save us, Uncle Zak."

Further out in the woods, the creatures had found a place to rest for a few minutes. The male was angry that he'd gotten shot, even though the bullet was not life-threatening. It made a two-inch gash about a quarter-inch deep, and the blood was running down his face. The female sat by his side and licked the blood away while attempting to stop its flow.

Chapter 41 - The Retribution

A flame thrower is an interesting tool and an even more exciting weapon. Amid the many uses, by far, the more twisted has to be that of a weapon. Used to clear brush, melt snow, clear old buildings and debris, it is highly effective. But turned on animal and human flesh, it is devastating. The propellant used has the consistency of napalm, and if anyone has seen history reels of the Vietnam war, it truly is devastating.

Sheriff Kane sat oiling his favorite weapon. His Smith and Wesson, pearl-handled, silver-plated 38 revolver was his go-to. Although not the one he carried in the line of duty, it would be worn on his hip on this trip. As he ran the barrel brush through the bore, his eyes glanced over at the portable M2A1 flamethrower, his secret weapon. It, too, would make this trip.

Zak placed his 45 automatic on the table and started to put things in his small duffel. He knew this hunt with Seth, Kane, and his small posse would be different. The determination that all the members had was at its peak, and they all knew they had to end this.

Seth opened Zak's front door and said, "You ready?"

Zak picked up his pistol and put it in its holster and grabbed his bag, and said, "let's go."

When they met Kane and the three men at the base of the mountain, all were pumped. The energy level was high, but they were veterans at the hunt and knew how to calm their excitement and focus on coming. The woods that day were bright and clear, and the view was good. Kane having strapped the portable flame thrower canister to his back and the gun portion hooked to the tank. But his weapon of choice was the 38 revolver that he held in his hand as they walked through the woods.

With his favorite hunting rifle, Seth moved through the woods with the group, eyes scanning as he walked. With his pistol at his side, Zak held a pump-action 12-gauge shotgun and moved along at the ready.

The group made their way to the cave entrance. Knowing this to be the creatures' mainstay area, they stood at alert and listened and looked for any sign of the two monsters.

Kane, thinking the best way to track his adversary, would be to enter the cave first and clear it before moving into the more open woods, shifted his pistol to its holster, and readied the gun of the flamethrower into his hands.

The creatures had retreated to the cave earlier with the female feasting on a small animal she'd caught, heard the humans' approach, and throwing the animal carcass aside, the female silently moved toward the entrance. Both Kane and the female met at the entrance simultaneously, and she lunged at him. Kane, in a moment of complete surprise, stepped forward and pulled the trigger of the gun. The nozzle spewed its napalm substance over the entire creature's body and engulfed her in flames as the creature slammed into Kane throwing both hard into the wall of the entrance of the cave. The canister hit the wall at Kane's back, and both creature and man exploded in a horrific fireball. The smoke inhalation, as well as extreme fire, was killing both Kane and the creature.

Zak, Seth, and the posse who had been outside the entrance could only watch in horror as the flames begin to die down to nothing to leave the charred remains of each. At the far end of the cave, the male creature seeing the massive fire engulfs his mate and erupts into the explosion, let out a horrific scream. He ran further into the cave and started to make his way to another passage leading out into the woods and higher mountains, yelling as he ran, knowing his mate was dead.

The members of the posse, having made a litter, gathered Kane's remains and made their way down from the mountain to their waiting vehicles.

As Zak got into his truck, he grabbed the steering wheel and feeling the pain of seeing his friend's death and the havoc the remaining creature would still do. He lifted his head to stare straight ahead and knew what he had to do with crystal clarity.

Chapter 42 – Zak's Mission

Zak had Dera and Kari stay with William in Seattle until he could give her the heads up that the female creature had been exterminated. He told her the male creature was still in the forest. He told her that he or Seth would go out every day, fed, and water their animals while they were gone.

As he sat on his sofa, he thought about how much he loved the Pacific Northwest and the Skokomish Wilderness and was hoping to raise his own family in Lilliwaup someday. But the serenity of his peaceful life had been jeopardized by two creatures that were interjected into the forest by Aliens. He was angry as he thought about what they had done, "For what, for some alien experiment?" He was saddened about the loss of Sheriff Kane but happy Kane had killed the female creature. She was nothing but a vicious and ruthless killer, just like her mate.

The huge male was angry and out for revenge. He was outraged about his mate's death and blamed Zak for it. He also hated Zak for shooting him in the head and trying to kill him. The creature would not sit silently in the wake of his mate's death as he went on his hunt for Zak.

It was around midnight when Zak was startled awake by the bone-chilling scream of the male creature. It was just inside the tree line and near his house. He had been watching Zak from the woods and found where he lived earlier in the day. After watching Zak all day, he knew he was home alone, but he also knew he had his guns and didn't want to be killed by them. He waited until the lights in Zak's house went out, and after waiting for about an hour, he couldn't wait any longer. He wanted to sneak up on Zak and kill him, but his anger overwhelmed him. He had instinctively let out his feeling with the scream, and it was too late to make a surprise attack, so he started moving swiftly toward the house.

When Zak first heard the scream, he immediately jumped out of bed, grabbed his rifle, and ran to the front door. He wasn't going to wait for the creature to break it down as he turned on his porch light and opened the door. The creature was coming out of the woods, grunting, and growling loudly, and it was moving toward him. The night was dark, but Zak could see the silhouette of the creature as it charged straight at him. Zak leveled his rifle and took aim, and as the shot rang out, the bullet's velocity knocked the creature backward and off his feet. Zak had only wounded the massive creature as it jumped back to its feet and took off running into the woods. It happened so quickly that Zak's second and third shots were missed as the creature meshed into the darkness. Unnerved and shaken, he stayed awake the rest of the night, with his weapons by his side, just in case the creature returned. As he lay there awake, he thought, "How did he find out where I lived?" Then the chilling truth hit him in the face, "He's been watching me."

The following day, he saw Seth and told him the creature came to his house in the middle of the night, and he shot and wounded him before it went back into the woods. He told Seth he was going to go out and find the creature and try to kill him. He believed he was the only one that should hunt down the wounded creature because he was the one with the experience and felt like it would be just like hunting down Shief in Afghanistan. He said, "Look, Seth, I need for you to stay here and keep everyone out of the woods, I'm going to go get that creature, and I don't need anyone else getting killed. We have already found out that the male creature is too smart for us to find and kill him when there's a group of us hunting him. He stays just one step ahead of us all the time, and this could take me some time to finish. It took me months to complete my mission with Shief, so do me a favor and don't tell Julie until I've been out there a few days.

The two men looked at each other with an understanding, and Seth knew Zak was right, as he replied, "just come back alive."

The following day Zak was up before the break of dawn and had all his equipment stuffed in his backpack. He carried his rifle and had his pistol in his belt. He didn't wear any cologne, aftershave lotion, or anything that had any odor where the creature could catch his scent. He had an entrenching tool to dig a hole and bury his feces and urine so the creature couldn't smell it. He didn't bring any food or water with him, choosing to live on what he could find in the forest. He put on his camouflaged clothes and painted his hands, neck, and face with black charcoal.

It was still early, and the sun was coming through the trees as he entered the forest. He moved along at a cautious clip until he got close to Sawtooth ridge and not far from where he believed the creature might be hiding.

That's when his entire demeanor changed. He started acting like the creature he was hunting; he separated his mind from his compassionate thinking and started thinking like a warrior on a mission to find his target.

As he started hunting, he stayed low to the ground, bending at the waist, and moved short distances very slowly at a time. He placed one foot in front of the other as he edged along. He would take several steps and then scan in all directions for any kind of movement. It was a slow, methodical process, but he knew it was the only way he could stay alive. By dark, he had only gotten about a half-mile from the Ridge and hadn't seen his enemy.

Before dark, he found a large fallen tree just off the trail and made a place where he could hide beneath it and get a little sleep for the night. He put on his night-vision goggles and watched the woods for several hours as he got a few cat naps during the night. He hadn't heard any screams from the creature the entire day or night, so he was beginning to wonder where he was. He began to think, "Maybe he's nurturing his wound or despondent about losing his mate?"

As he sat there alone in the dark, he whispered, "Man, you got to be a little crazy to be out here in these wood with that wounded creature on the loose. If it finds you, it'll kill you and eat you." He could hear the thumping of his heartbeat and mice scurrying across the leaves as he occasionally glanced up at the millions of stars in the sky. It was an eerie feeling, feeling like he was the only person in the world, except for the monster out there somewhere.

He was moving around early the following day and determined he was going to find his target. He listened for anything that sounded like the creature knocking or screaming. It was silent, except for an occasional bird that squawked in the trees. As he made his way deeper into the forest, there were a few areas where there were thirty yards of open space, so being extra cautious not to be seen, he low crawled across to the other side.

As he got a little closer to the cave entrance, he set up a noose trap by bending a good size tree he could bend into a half-circle and placed a hidden rope, with a noose at the end to try and catch the creature and raise it in the air by one leg. Further up, he bent a tree on the trail and placed a tripwire to it with sharp stakes ready to snap back and sink deep into the creature's body. The entire time he moved around slowly and was vigilant, he scanned for any sign of the creature trying to sneak upon him.

He spent the entire day setting up different traps for the creature, but there's still was no sign of him. Once the traps were set, he detoured a small waterfall and got some much-needed water. He was able to get a few fish with a makeshift spear and ate the fish raw. He washed the fish smell from his hands with mud and plants from the edge of the creek. He found an empty cave hole in the side of the creek wall just large enough for him to take refuge in for the night. He again kept a vigilant eye open for the creature with his night goggles. During his second night, he looked up at the stars. He thought, "Damn, I'd much rather be home in bed with Julie instead of doing this." The reality of this mission was that he had to kill the creature to protect her.

It was the middle of the third day when he finally got a glimpse of the wounded creature, and he was limping along on the trail and toward Sawtooth Ridge. It was too far from him for Zak to get a shot, so he moved quickly toward the creature's hideout and cave entrance. Once there, he set up three claymore mines he had gotten from a few of his Army friends. He placed them just outside the entrance to the cave and ran wires from the claymores about thirty yards away from where he would be hiding in a hole, along with the trigger to set them off. He had them pointed outward and covered them with leaves, so he could blow up the creature as he started to go into the cave.

It was late in the night when the creature finally returned to the cave entrance, but he was now cautious as he slowly limped up close to the entrance. Zak knew he was smart and figured he had already encountered his other traps and somehow avoided them. Zak thought, "That bastard is smart and knows I'm after him."

As he got close to the entrance, he realized something was not right, so he stopped and looked around for a second, then quickly turned around as if he was going to flee. Then Zak pushed the trigger, and three loud explosions went off and hit the creature up and down its back and legs, and the shrapnel sunk deep into the creature's body. He went down as he let out a loud, huge, painful scream. Zak then quickly fired four shots from his rifle in his direction and hit him in the upper chest area and his left arm with two of the bullets. Zak was surprised, the creature got to his feet again and started limping toward the mountains' upper parts. It disappeared into the darkness. Zak whispered, "Damn, that thing must have nine lives, just like a cat?"

Zak knew it was not the time to follow the creature into the mountains, it was too dark, and the creature had the advantage, even though it was wounded. He found a place to hide for the rest of the night but didn't sleep. He figured an injured creature was like an injured bear and more dangerous than anything, so he had to be on guard if it came looking for him. He used his night-vision goggles the rest of the night if the creature tried to sneak up on him.

The sun was coming up over the mountains when he crawled out of his hiding place. It was now the fourth day of his hunt as he rose to go after his wounded target. He began to follow the creature's drying blood up into the mountains. Just as he got close to the upper mountain cave entrance, the creature came charging at him from behind a large rock, but he was weak from his wounds and losing blood. He couldn't mount the typical furious assault as he would've typically done, but he knocked Zak to the ground, and his rifle went flying. He tried to come at Zak but staggered and almost fell as he opened his mouth and showed Zak his long fangs. Zak knew he was still strong enough to kill him if he got his massive arms around him, so Zak quickly got to his feet and reached for his pistol in his waistband. He promptly fired four shots at the creature from about twelve feet away, hitting him two more times in the upper body as the monster went down again. This time it wasn't springing back to its feet, like before.

The creature was still breathing, and Zak could see that he was dying. Suddenly a huge spacecraft flew in quickly and stopped abruptly above the flailing beast. Zak could only watch in amazement as a door opened, and light shot down, and the creature was lifted upward and inside. The door closed, and the craft shot through the sky, punching a perfect circle through the clouds.

Zak let out a tremendous yell, "We got you!" And then fell to one knee and, looking up, softly added, "don't come back."

Chapter 43 – The Resolution

It didn't take long, and everyone in the community found out the creatures were no longer a threat. They heard about Sheriff Kane killing the female creature and Zak getting rid of the male. However, Zak never told anyone except Julie and Seth that the aliens had picked up the male creature after being shot several times and hardly breathing. He just told everyone it was gone and wouldn't be back. People were no longer afraid to come out of their homes.

A few days after Walker's tribe got the news about the two creatures, they were happy they no longer had to be on guard from them. Walker decided to visit Seth on a Sunday morning. Seth was kicking back, relaxing on the sofa, watching football, when he got the knock on his door. When he opened the front door, staring him right in the face, was a two-month-old puppy that Walker was holding up in the air. It looked at Seth and let out a light growl.

Walker laughed and said, "Damn, this puppy is just like his older cousin Rex; he doesn't like anyone either. But he is yours now, so you have to deal with him." He told Seth he was from the same mother and father as Rex. He chuckled and said, "He and Rex must be cousins, just like you and Zak."

Seth reached for the puppy and cuddled him in his arms, and rubbed his neck as he said, "Wow!" Thank you, Walker, that's the best gift ever. He looks just like Rex." Seth had a huge smile on his face as he looked at Walker and said, "I think I'll call this boy Max."

Driving up to Julie's house Zak was happy. Not only were the creature monsters gone, but Zak felt his demons were now gone as well. Julie grabbed Zak hard and embraced him, and gave him a passionate kiss. Seth had broken down and finally told Julie of Zac's mission when he had not returned after a while.

"How about lunch on me?" Julie said.

Zak nodded. "Bessie's ok?" she replied.

"Absolutely," Zak said. As they got into Julie's car and Zak said, "Hey, I like this, you being so lovey-dovey and all, I could get used to this."

"Whoa, slow down, mister," Julie laughed as she started the car.

Making their way toward Bessie's Diner, Julie seemed to be lost in thought. "Is this what brings Zak calm, the hunt, the chase? Death and destruction? No, that's not my Zak."

Zak was lost in the thoughts of his own as his memory wandered back to the last hunt he and his grandfather had taken before he deployed to Afghanistan. "Grandpa, I need you to do this for me and help take care of Julie if I don't make it back from over there. I love her so much."

John turned to his grandson and said: "Zak, you are smart, and you'll be fine, and you will come back. THE LOVE OF THAT WOMAN WILL BRING YOU BACK."

As they pulled into Bessie's parking lot, Zak was drawn back to reality and softly mouthed, "Thank you, Grandpa." Julie turned off her car's engine, and Zak turned to Julie and said, "Yes, I could get used to this and know that ALL the monsters are gone. I'll need you more than ever."

Julie looking down, looked up at Zak, and smiling said, "Let's have a baby." and Zak smiled.

Epilogue:

Having once again entered the dark vastness of space, the alien craft made its way toward the next waiting planet. The large male creature on the verge of death lay on a huge gleaming metallic-like table. The aliens moved closer to begin their examination and dissection, which would reveal the true motive of their creations as one alien said, "It looks like we got our answer. Even in the forests' remote region, when threatened, it only took the humans 96 days to kill our two test animals. Now we know just how aggressive and brutal in nature the humans truly are."

Sources of Information:

Mount Skokomish Wilderness
https://en.wikipedia.org – mount_skokomish_wilderness

Olympic National Park
www.fs.usda.gov>recarea>olympia>recarea

Genetic analysis of hair samples attributed to Yeti, Bigfoot
https://royalsocietypublishing.org>doi>pdf>rspb.2014.0161
sykes@wolfsonox.ac.uk.

Wikipedia - Nanotechnology

https://en.wikipedia.org – nanotechnology

I want to give a special thanks to Rita Toews for developing the book's cover for us.

Rita Toews of www.yourebookcover.com

Other books by Ron L. Carter:

Twenty-One Months – non-fiction
From the Darkness of my Mind – fiction
American Terrorist – A Grandfather's Revenge - fiction
American Terrorist – The Revenge Continues - fiction
Night Crawlers – fiction
Night Crawlers – Reign of Terror - fiction
Unearthly Realms – fiction
Accidental Soldiers – fiction
Zak Thomas – The Monster Hunter
Love me now, Don't wait - Poetry

Made in the USA
Middletown, DE
07 October 2022

12108875R00090